Creamy and Overflowing

9 Lactation Erotica Short Stories

Adriana Gala

Copyright

Table of Contents

Lactation Erotica Short Story

Doctor helps me with my Milky Breasts

Creamy 1

and Overflowing

Adriana Gala

Doctor Helps Me with My Milky Breasts

Creamy and Overflowing 1

At 19 years old, I thought I knew my body, but one day my breasts suddenly started hurting. They were swollen and hard, just touching them caused me pain, it hurt to even put my bra on. And if that wasn't enough, then I noticed how my soft cotton blouse had two wet circles on it. Milk was dripping from my nipples!

Naturally, I was scared. This had never happened to me before. So I called Dr. Mendoza's office. Luckily, his secretary was able to make an appointment for me that afternoon, so at 4:30 pm I was sitting in the waiting room.

I put on a jacket and a clean blouse over my bra, but I felt that that last garment was strangling my now hypersensitive breasts. I would have preferred not to wear it, but I developed at an early age and was the first of my friends to have boobs; it also turned out that I have huge boobs, so going without a bra is not something that can be easily overlooked in my case. I had always thought of my bust as my best attribute, but right now I felt like I had two stones the size of melons on my chest.

I was flipping through a magazine while I waited for my appointment; apart from Miss Allen, the secretary, I was the only patient in the waiting area. Apparently I was the last appointment of the day.

I heard the door open and an older man with a cane came out of the office. Miss Allen told me that I could go in now.

Dr. Mendoza's office was nice. He had a desk with a computer, a bookcase full of huge books with unpronounceable names. His numerous diplomas were framed on the wall, and an oriental style divider separated that space from the examination area.

I sat in one of the chairs in front of his desk and waited for the doctor to arrive. He entered through a door at the other end of his office.

Dr. Mendoza is the kind of man who becomes more handsome with age. I think he must be like 45 or 46 years old. He wears glasses and his dark hair is tinged with gray, together with his handsome features and muscular build, he is a very sexy, older man. He has a broad back and toned arms, it is evident that he is in very good shape as I notice his muscles under his clothes. And in addition to his good looks, he has always been a kind and attentive person; he's not like other doctors who do not even look at you and seem like they can't wait until you leave their office. Dr. Mendoza listens carefully and asks many questions in order to make a good diagnosis.

Upon seeing me, he recognized me immediately and greeted me with a kind smile.

"Hello Veronica. How are you? What brings you here?"

"Hi Dr. Mendoza," I looked at him and a wave of shame washed over me, I lowered my eyes and replied "Okay... more or less."

He sat behind his desk and took off his glasses, "What's up Veronica?"

"Uuummmmm…" I couldn't find the words.

At that moment the phone on his desk rang. He picked it up, "Yes?" After a moment he replied,

"It's okay Sophie. No problem at all. Veronica is the last patient today, so you can go and get to your son's game. See you tomorrow. Goodbye."

After hanging up the phone, he stood up and walked over to where I was standing. He sat on the other chair next to me and placed his hand on my knee.

"It's alright Veronica. You know you can tell me anything, and whatever it is, I promise it won't leave this office."

"This is difficult to explain..."

He gave me another kind smile.

"Well... my breasts hurt."

He nodded.

"Are you having discomfort with PMS or your period?"

I giggled nervously.

"I wish that was it." I plucked up my courage and took off my jacket. "You see; my breasts feel as heavy as rocks. They are extremely sensitive, and on top of that, they're dripping milk."

Dr. Mendoza only raised his eyebrows and looked at my huge breasts and the new wet circles that stained my blouse. I didn't know if it was possible, but they seemed to be even larger than usual.

After a minute he looked at my face and said, "Come on over to exam area, Veronica. Sit on the table and we'll see what's going on."

I stood up and walked over to the examination area; with the help of a small footstool I sat on the table and waited for the doctor to diagnose my mysterious condition.

"Please take off your blouse and bra, Veronica."

I did as he asked and breathed a sigh of relief as I released them. My nipples were hard and on each tip was a drop of white milk.

"May I?" Asked the doctor, indicating that he was going to touch my bare chest.

I looked down in embarrassment, feeling the heat creep up my cheeks.

"Sure Doctor," I replied.

It didn't make sense for me to feel that way, he had been my family's doctor all my life. I had known him since I was a child. It wasn't the first time that he examined me, but as soon as I felt his warm hand on my chest, a shudder ran through my body and a pleasant tingling awakened between my legs.

He wrapped both hands around one of my big tits and began to apply pressure, I whimpered in pain.

"Does it hurt when I do this to you?" He gently squeezed my breast again.

I frowned and nodded.

He touched my areola and pressed from the base of my nipple towards the tip. A thin stream of milk shot out and landed on his cheek. This took us both by surprise and I gasped in mortification. I put my hands over my face and wished with all my might that the earth would swallow me whole, but instead of being disgusted or something like that, Dr. Mendoza chuckled.

"Sorry, sorry, sorry," I said humiliated. I felt so ashamed that tears burned my eyes and threatened to overflow.

When the doctor's concentration returned to me,

his amused expression changed to a serious one at seeing me so distraught.

"You have nothing to apologize for, Veronica," he said, resting his hands on my shoulders and looking at my face.

"B ... but ... I ..." I sputtered pointing to his face.

What the doctor did next stunned me.

"This?" He said and put his hand to his cheek where my milk had wet his face; he wiped the milk with his fingers and brought them to his mouth. The tip of his tongue poked between his lips and he licked my milk from his fingers.

"This is nothing to be ashamed of, Veronica. It seems to me that your case is simply Spontaneous Lactation. It's nothing to worry about. It is something that happens to some women even though they are not pregnant or have had children.

What is important is that you express your milk, that's why you have pain in your breasts. Right now they're loaded with milk and you need to release the pressure.

I noticed how his eyes sparkled while he spoke,

with what?… Desire?

"And how do I get the milk out?"

"You can buy a breast pump. There are manual and electric ones, you can find them in any maternity store or buy one online. You can express the milk by hand as well."

He picked up a metal bowl from the table that held his various instruments, brought it to my breast and placed it under my nipple.

I gasped when I felt the cold metal touch my skin.

"Sorry," he said, "I forgot to warn you that it would be cold. Especially now that your chest is so sensitive."

All this was very strange, I didn't know what to think, but I couldn't deny that my heart was beating rapidly in my chest. I felt the moisture of my sex soaking my underwear and I longed more than anything to feel the hands of Dr. Mendoza on my tits.

"Use any convenient container to collect the milk. Massage them or take a hot shower to help get the milk flowing, then squeeze from the base towards the tip of the nipple, like I did, to release the milk.

The doctor was massaging my breast and squeezing my nipple, effectively milking me. I closed my eyes and I think I groaned with pleasure, because moments later the doctor's voice brought me out of the pleasant haze of sensation.

"There's another way too," he said.

I opened my eyes and looked at him, I could see in his eyes the same desire that was now rushing through me.

"What?" I asked.

"I said... there is also another way ... to express your milk."

"How?"

"Like this ..." He put the metal bowl back on the table and leaned his head towards my chest. I felt his breath on my wet nipple and then a rush of ecstasy ran through my body as he wrapped his lips around it and sucked. My nipples were hypersensitive and seemed to have a direct connection to my clit, which was now flickering with excitement. Without thinking, I ran my fingers through his hair and pressed his face against the breast he was sucking. A groan rumbled in his chest, my action assured him that I liked what he was doing, so he drank my milk with big, loud gulps.

As he continued to suck my breast, they began to soften. He was sucking out all the milk that had built up inside them, and in the process of relieving my pain, he awakened a hot wave of desire inside me.

"Oh, yes! Yes, please! Please suck it all out, Doctor! It feels so much better when you suck it! Please, do the other one too!"

The doctor turned his attention to my other breast, which was still rock hard. He first teased my nipple, flicking it with the tip of his tongue. He squeezed gently with his hands and a stream of milk gushed from my nipple and fell into his open mouth. After catching a few squirts like that, he reached over, covered my nipple with his lips and sucked, gently at first, just as he had done with the other, but as soon as he felt my hands in his hair again, crushing his face against my tits, he gripped me more confidently and firmly, certain that he had drunk enough that I no longer felt any pain.

"Your milk tastes so sweet, Veronica. You're delicious." He murmured while he drank from one breast, then the other.

My hands explored the expansion of his back and shoulders; I moaned, consumed by the pleasure that his mouth provoked on my tits, I didn't want him to stop... ever.

"Please, doctor. Don't stop… I feel..."

He pulled away from my tits for a moment and his eyes were full of lust. He crashed his mouth against mine in a passionate kiss. I savored the warm, sweet milk that he transferred from his mouth to mine. It was such a perverse, erotic, and intimate act that my hips swayed, yearning to feel more of him than only his mouth on my tits.

"We shouldn't be doing this, Veronica. But I can't seem to help myself. If you want me to stop, I will. But God help me, I want to fuck you so bad!"

"Please fuck me! I want to feel you inside me!"

He kissed me again while he unbuttoned my jeans. He then broke away to remove my shoes and finish undressing me, leaving me completely naked on the table. Then he proceeded to take off his clothes. When he was naked in front of me, I wrapped my hand around his hard cock, stroking his length. He moaned and surrounded my waist, lifting me into his arms; I wrapped my legs around him as he turned around and sat on the exam table. On top of him, I rose on my knees, found his hard cock with my hand and guided it to my entrance. My pussy was dripping wet and his cock inched his way inside, stretching my tight entrance around his thickness.

I rode him slowly at first, enjoying the fullness of him inside me. In the time that he had stopped sucking on my boobs, the milk hadn't stopped flowing from my nipples; so white streams of milk ran down from my breasts over my belly.

He had placed us in the perfect position, sitting on top of him my chest was at the level of his face and he wasted no time latching on to my wet nipples again, drinking the sweet liquid as he thrust upward, burying himself deep within my pussy.

I arched my back, pressing my large tits into his face as my hips rocked back and forth, my clit rubbing against his pelvis, driving me crazy with desire.

The more he sucked my milky breasts and fucked my pussy, the faster I rocked my hips on top of him. Each thrust of his cock made me more wanton. The rhythm of our fused bodies had become frantic and my ass slapped noisily on his thighs. I was riding him harder and harder; my moans grew as I felt my orgasm reach the point of no return. My climax washed over me, unleashing an electric blast supercharged from the most intense pleasure I had ever experienced in my short life.

The orgasm took over my body, contracting all my muscles; meanwhile, the doctor held on my tits with a firm grasp, he squeezed them and bathed his face and his chest with jets of milk that sprayed out of my nipples with each orgasmic contraction.

My pussy squeezed and tightened around his hard cock, taking him with me to the edge of ecstasy; I felt his cock swell inside me moments before shooting his thick white cum deep inside me.

We were panting, my arms and legs around him, his face resting against my breasts.

"How do you feel?" the doctor asked.

"Much better than when I arrived doctor," I answered with a smile.

He kissed me on the lips, the sweet taste of my milk still permeating his breath.

"I am very happy to help you. Whenever you need assistance in relieving the pressure in your breasts, you can always come to me," he said with a mischievous glint in his eyes.

I grinned. "And how often do you think I will need to express my milk?"

"Maybe every day at first; But later, when your body gets used to it, you can go more days without feeling the swelling in your breasts. It may be every three days after that."

"And are you sure you can see me so many times?"

"As many times as you need. My duty is to serve you," he said, winking at me. "But I can't deny it's a pleasure to help you with this situation."

THE END

Creamy 2
and Overflowing
Lactation Erotica Short Story
Both my Bosses
want to Drink my Milk
Adriana Gala

Both my Bosses want to Drink my Milk

Creamy and Overflowing 2

I was sitting in one of the chairs in front of my boss's desk. The office was alone, as everyone else was downstairs in the restaurant, eating and celebrating the CEO's birthday.

The company where I work is a transnational construction company with good salaries, benefits and excellent treatment of its employees. The bosses make sure we are all well taken care of, and that includes hosting parties and events beyond the typical annual Christmas dinner.

I work as an Executive Assistant to the Director of Public Relations; he is an intelligent, kind, and very attractive man. Since I returned to work after my maternity leave, Mr. Oliveira, my boss, made a very kind gesture by offering me the privacy of his office to express my milk. With his characteristic sympathy, he respectfully informed me that I could enjoy the privacy and comfort of his office to carry out my personal maternal needs. His gesture inspired deep gratitude in me, as well as amazement, since I thought he was going to scold me for regularly being absent from my desk, sometimes up to 20 minutes at a time when I needed to go to the ladies' room to pump my milk.

A few days after I'd come back to work, he had called me into his office and said "With all due respect Victoria, have you been feeling well since you've been back?"

"Yes, Mr. Oliveira," I answered nervously. I hadn't explained the reason for my long stays in the bathroom, even though I tried to carry them out most of the time during my lunch break. But there were times when I needed to express my milk more than once, otherwise I felt like my breasts were going to burst. And if I didn't, I had already discovered that the excess milk was spilling from my nipples, soaking through the breast pads I used in my bra and leaving two wet circles on my blouse, which I consequently hid by putting on the jacket I wore to the office.

"It's just that since you've been back, I couldn't help noticing that you disappear for long periods of time into the ladies' room, and I wanted to make sure that you're well. If you need more time after the birth of your child, I'm sure we can arrange something. You are an invaluable employee, both to me and to the company."

"Thank you, Mr. Oliveira, you and the company have been incredibly generous and understanding. I apologize if I have worried you or you think that I haven't fulfilled my duties. You see... My trips to the ladies' room are because I need to... Uh... express the milk from my breasts for my baby."

A quick flash of heat shone in his eyes as a look of understanding came upon him; and then he frowned.

"I don't mean to pry… but, can that be done in a bathroom?"

"Well... It's not ideal, and it's a bit awkward to tell you the truth." But it's not something I can do at my desk, since I need some privacy," I said without looking up from my hands folded on my lap.

"Well, I think it's my duty to ensure that you have an adequate environment to do this. Since there is no room for it in the common space of the office around your colleagues, I insist that you use my office. Here you will have the privacy you need, as well as a more comfortable space. You are the only person with the second key, so feel free to come in here when I'm out in a meeting. And if I'm here, just ask me if I want some milk with my tea," he grinned and went on, "I'll go downstairs to the cafe and you'll have your privacy while I take a little break from all this work. It will be our secret password," He said, winking at me.

I was dumbfounded.

"Thank you, sir; but I can't bother you like that."

"Not at all Victoria, what's more, from this moment on I forbid you to do that anywhere else but here while you're at work. Being a mother is sacred, and women who sacrifice for their children deserve the utmost respect."

I thanked him and retired to my cubicle with a smile on my face. I undoubtedly had the best boss in the world.

Several weeks passed and things flowed very naturally. Sure, at that time I never used the password he had offered me, but Mr. Oliveira is such a perceptive man that he surely noticed the change in my posture or in my gestures, because when my breasts felt like rocks on my chest, he would stop by my desk and inform me that he would be absent for a while, since he wanted some milk in his tea. And having been his assistant for three years now, I knew that he didn't take any milk with his tea.

On this particular day when the entire office was celebrating the CEO's birthday, I stayed behind to pump my milk behind closed doors in my boss's office. I was starting to fill the bottle, the shield positioned over my swollen breast and the buzzing of my electric breast pump starting to draw the milk from my nipple, the white liquid flowing down the tubes to the small container when the familiar sucking sensation stopped. Abruptly.

I hit the switch several times, but the device wouldn't turn on. Then I noticed that the cable wasn't properly plugged in. I got up from the chair, my blouse unbuttoned, my breasts dripping milk, and as I tried to fit it into the outlet, I heard the office door open and close behind me. I got up and was paralyzed when I saw my boss, accompanied by the Project Coordination Manager, Mr. Da Silva.

They were chatting animatedly until they noticed my presence. Their gazes dropped from my face with an alarmed expression and were riveted on my exposed breasts, connected to the machine to express the milk from my engorged breasts.

After several seconds, which seemed like an eternity, I was able to react enough to remove the shield, I held it with one hand while the other closed the blouse over my chest. But it was just my luck that I hadn't managed to pump more than a few minutes, and since they were already stimulated by the suction of the machine, in a few moments my white blouse was soaked, making the thin fabric completely see through, my erect nipples perfectly visible in the eyes of my bosses.

My face must have become bright red; I could feel the heat of my shame creeping like fire up my cheeks finding myself in this situation. I started spluttering apologies.

"Mr. Oliveira, excuse me, I thought you were downstairs at the party. I didn't know that you would be back with Mr. Da Silva so soon."

"You have nothing to apologize for, Victoria," he said without taking his eyes off my now transparent blouse due to the amount of milk that flowed from my nipples.

Then Mr. Da Silva spoke.

"I wish I could apologize to Victoria, but finding you like this is the most sensual thing I've seen in years."

Da Silva's comment confused me, and he surely saw that confusion on my face because he continued. "There is nothing more seductive than a voluptuous woman, and nothing more delicious than the milk that flows from her body. I was lucky enough to try it with my daughter's mother, and they were the most exciting experiences of my life. Would it be too much to ask to try a little of that sweet milk from your beautiful tits?"

A part of me said that I should be outraged by what this man had just said to me, but on the other hand, hearing him speak to me in that way, respectful and naughty at the same time, I felt a tingling between my legs that I hadn't felt in a long time.

I am a single mother, and the only good thing the father of my child had given me was my baby. So standing in front of these two powerful and masculine men, I was delightfully pleased to find that they wanted me that way.

The shame that had seized me waned to give way to a dark and sensual desire that took hold of me.

"Victoria, you don't have to do anything you don't want to do, but I can't deny that what Da Silva said is absolutely true. You're the most sensual woman I've ever known, and seeing you like this is so tempting."

I looked at my two bosses, strong men who could easily take whatever they wanted; but they were giving me a choice, they were inviting me to a physical encounter that I would never have imagined. The desire in their gaze, along with the unmistakable bulge that pressed against their trousers, washed away any moral reasoning from my mind. I wanted to succumb to this feeling, to be seduced by this desire. I placed the breast shield near the pump and let my blouse hang open, revealing my naked breasts, loaded with so much milk that white drops bloomed on my nipples.

Seeing my response, Oliveira locked the door and both men approached me.

They each tilted their heads and I felt their lips enveloping my nipples. When they started sucking, arousal shot through me like lightning. As my bosses drank the milk from my tits, I felt the moisture between my legs ooze out of me, soaking my underwear.

I arched my back, my hands holding the head of each man suckling my engorged tits, drinking the milk from my breasts.

Once my breasts had become softer, I felt Da Silva's hand slide under my skirt. His fingers brushed the wet fabric of my thong before pushing it aside and penetrating my pussy, invading my slick channel with his finger.

"You're so wet," he murmured against my breast, teasing my nipple with his tongue.

Oliveira detached himself from my tit and kissed my mouth with such wild intensity that I thought I would cum right in that moment. His lips against mine, his tongue in my mouth, I could taste the sweet flavor of my milk on his breath.

I had been leaning against the desk, and before I sat on it, Da Silva pulled my skirt up until it was bunched up around my hips, he then slid my thong down my legs and took off my underwear. I was sitting on the hard wooden surface when Da Silva spread my legs, leaving my sex fully exposed to his hungry mouth. His tongue licked my slit, drinking the cream of my arousal; but it was when Oliveira was squeezing my tits and pinching my nipples, that Da Silva's mouth swirled on clit, licking my hard pink nub relentlessly while Oliveira milked me with his mouth and hands, making me moan loudly as I started to cum.

I couldn't contain the moans or the shaking of my body, but the most impressive thing was that while the currents of pleasure electrocuted each one of my cells, with each spasm of my climax, jets of milk shot from my nipples like a white fountain, bathing my chest, my abdomen and Oliveira's face with the sweet liquid.

As the intensity of the orgasm diminished, the jets of milk weakened. When my milk stopped spilling, my bosses got naked. Da Silva lifted me off the desk and lay down on the floor, positioning me on his erection. I could feel him filling me with his swollen cock, inch by inch, until he buried himself to the hilt in my wet pussy. My big tits were hanging over his face and he wasted no time in wrapping one of my erect nipples in his mouth and sucking it. Every time one of them stimulated my breasts, it was as if the pleasure between my legs doubled, I began to ride him while he sucked one tit and then the other, my soft tits bouncing on his face.

When I arched my back and looked up, I saw Oliveira standing over us, stroking his hard cock. Without exchanging words, I parted my lips, inviting him to penetrate my mouth with his sex, and that was how my two bosses were fucking me at the same time. Oliveira was fucking my face, burying his length to the back of my throat while Da Silva filled my pussy with his fat cock and licked and sucked my tits, drinking the white milk that flowed from them and dripped onto his face. The encounter was so erotic and naughty that I was already going to cum again. I moaned around Oliveira's cock sliding in and out of my mouth, letting his length drown out my moans of pleasure; and Da Silva squeezed my ass with his hands, rocking my hips harder while he kept thrusting in and out of my pussy as it clenched rhythmically around his thickness.

I wasn't the only one who couldn't hold back any longer, I felt Da Silva's cock pulse inside me as he shot jets of thick white cum deep inside my pussy, groaning while he drank the thin streams of milk that surged from my nipples matching the rhythm of my climax.

As soon as Da Silva had finished emptying his seed within me, Oliveira withdrew his cock from my mouth and said something in Portuguese that I only half understood; then Da Silva rolled our bodies, laying my back on the floor with my legs spread, my slit dripping with the combination of our juices. I felt the emptiness of their absence, when seconds ago they had filled me at both ends, but then Oliveira knelt between my legs, and without caring that his colleague had filled me to the brim with his cum, he buried his cock deeply in my pussy, filling me again with his length. His thrusts were intense and fast, my sex was hypersensitive from so much stimulation, so when he rubbed my clit with his fingers, my body contracted and another orgasm burst from my core, pulling a cry of desperate pleasure from my lips as each peak of pleasure that ran through my body prompted another jet of warm milk to shoot out of my tits. Oliveira would not stop speaking to me in Portuguese, all the time continuing to rub my clit and squeeze my breasts, squeezing out more of the sweet nectar that initially seduced these men. I had no idea if he was calling me his whore or his goddess, but I didn't care, hearing him speak to me with that intensity in his language excited me, and I knew from his tone of voice that he was imprisoned by the passion of our encounter, and that his body buried in mine was causing that. He was repeating the same word over and over again until he groaned; he held me firmly by the thighs, keeping my legs open for him as he impaled me with brutal force and emptied his seed inside me, my sex now flooded with the cum of my two bosses.

When he finished, he leaned into my body, ran his tongue across my abdomen, savoring the remains of the milk from my tits, then sucking on each nipple and finally kissing me on the lips.

After the kiss, he withdrew his cock from my body and between the two of them they helped me stand up. I was disheveled, my clothes wrinkled and full of cum, sweat, and milk; but I didn't care, I felt radiant and satisfied, wickedly pleased to notice that the evidence of our encounter was running down the inner part of my thighs.

THE END

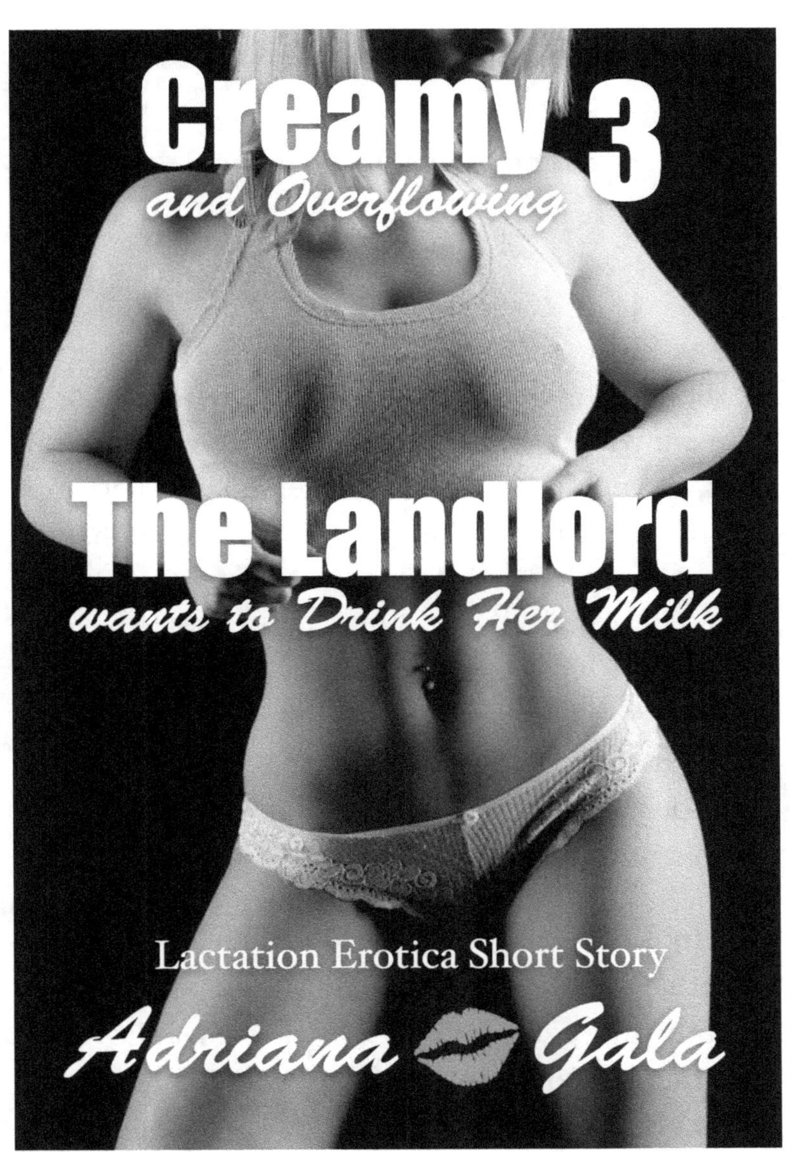

Creamy 3
and Overflowing
The Landlord
wants to Drink Her Milk
Lactation Erotica Short Story
Adriana Gala

The Landlord Wants to Drink Her Milk

Creamy and Overflowing 3

Ariana kicked off her heels as soon as she closed the door behind her. She had come from another failed interview. She leaned her head against the door, covered her face with her hands, and took several deep breaths to regain control of herself and not end up in a pool of tears. She couldn't afford that, she had to find a good job, otherwise she and her daughter would end up on the street.

The last think she was expecting was to feel her Landlord greedily drinking the milk that filled her tits that afternoon.

She took off her formal clothes to change into something more comfortable. She barely released her bra, squeezed both of her breasts, relieved to free them. Her nipples were beaded with white drops. Before making the cakes that she had to bake for that weekend, she should empty herself a bit to ease the pressure.

She was walking topless through the apartment,

getting ready to pump the milk she stored for her baby girl when the doorbell rang. She picked up a loose fitting top hanging on the back of the couch and quickly pulled it over her head before looking through the peep hole. When she saw Mr. Garcia, she opened the door, her stomach in knots.

"Hello, Mr. Garcia," she said as she opened the door and looked down in shame.

"Ariana, please call me Lorenzo. You've been living here for four years; we don't need to be so formal. Mr. Garcia makes me sound like an old man!" he said before adding. "Can I come in?"

"Of course. Please, come in," and gestured her Landlord to come into the apartment. Mr. Garcia sat in one of the chairs in front of the dining room table and Ariana asked, "Can I get you some tea or coffee?"

"Yes, some coffee would be nice. As long as you have milk and sugar, otherwise I don't like the taste." Ariana smiled, feeling a little bit more at ease in the presence of her landlord.

Lorenzo Garcia owned the building where she had been living the past four years. Her apartment was modest, but it was in a nice part of town. She had moved there with her now ex-boyfriend, but her relationship had come to a rather bitter end when she told Francisco that she was pregnant. She should have guessed from his expression the moment she gave him the news. As the days passed, they had several heated discussions, until one afternoon, when she came home from the office, she noticed that several things were missing.

The first thing she noticed was the absence of the flat screen TV. At first she thought that a thief had broken in, but upon examining a little more, she discovered that all of Francisco's belongings had disappeared.

Angry tears ran down her cheeks when she read his note: I'm not ready for this.

After seeing that Francisco was such an irresponsible coward, she promised herself that she would never cry for him again and that it was better for her and her baby not to have someone like that in their lives.

The life of a single mother wasn't easy, but she loved her little girl with all her heart, and all her hard work and sacrifice was done with pleasure to meet the needs of her daughter and herself. But once again she was facing a difficult chapter in her life. Three months ago she had lost her job. She immediately went into action and managed to sell home baked goods for children's parties, mainly for the children of the other mothers that she knew from the nursery where they took care of her daughter while she worked. However, that small income did not cover all of her expenses. Mr. Garcia was a man who had always treated her with kindness; and now, under her new circumstances, he was being very considerate by letting her live there the last three months without paying rent.

When Ariana placed the cup of coffee with milk and sugar on the table, she sat across from him on the opposite chair in the dining room; she felt her shoulders slump with shame, since she still didn't have even a third of the sum that she owed him.

Lorenzo took a sip of the hot drink, and smiled, making a pleased sound.

"You know exactly how I like it, Ariana. Thank you." But then the kind smile faded from his face and his expression turned serious. "How have you been Ariana? Do you and Irene have everything you need?"

Always so considerate, Ariana thought. Instead of asking me if I have the money I owe him, he first wants to know if we need anything.

She was mortified, she didn't want to be in debt to this man. Who, although he was incredibly generous, surely needed the money that she owed him. She had to find a way to repay him, she was amazed that he hadn't kicked her out yet.

With so many thoughts stumbling over each other in her head, Ariana didn't say anything, she just shook her head and pressed her hands against her eyes.

She heard the sound of his chair moving and a moment later she felt a large warm hand tentatively touch her knee. Lorenzo had knelt in front of her and was looking at her with concern. When their eyes met, he asked her, "What's wrong Ariana? Do you need something for Irene? I can loan you the money if you need it."

"No, no, thank you Mr. Garcia."

"Lorenzo. Please, call me Lorenzo," he interrupted.

Ariana took a deep breath and nodded.

"Okay… Lorenzo. Thanks. But it isn't that. And, I think I couldn't bear to take your money on top of what I already owe you. Fortunately, the sales I make from baking are covering most of my expenses, except... rent. I'm so embarrassed, I don't know why you haven't evicted us yet, anyone else would have."

"What kind of person would do that?" Lorenzo replied. "What kind of man would I be if I kicked out a single mother and her baby while going through a difficult time?"

Ariana couldn't help smiling upon hearing his words. Without a doubt this man was an angel sent from heaven.

"I think you just might be my guardian angel, Lorenzo."

He smirked, "Nah! I'm nowhere good enough to be an angel."

"I don't know how to thank you for letting us live here. That keeps me awake at night... the idea that Irene and I have nowhere to go."

Lorenzo looked at Ariana's face, contemplated her almond shaped eyes and her pink mouth that seemed to invite him to come closer and taste her. Being so close to her he could smell her rose and honey fragrance. When his eyes glanced at her generous bosom under her shirt, he noticed two wet circles. His reaction was immediate. Luckily, his position didn't reveal the erection that was now pressing against his trousers.

He had already lost count of the number of times he had masturbated to the thought of tasting the sweet milk that flowed from her large breasts. Lorenzo had never been married or had children, but he had always had a titillating curiosity and longing to be with a lactating woman. He had sometimes seen her at the park on weekends, discreetly breastfeeding her daughter, an involuntary desire awakened his imagination, and he visualized how it would feel to squeeze, kiss, and suck those voluptuous tits full of milk.

He must have been staring at her chest, because Ariana looked down where Lorenzo was staring and immediately was overcome with a new wave of humiliation.

"Oh, Lorenzo!" Her tone of voice revealing her

embarrassment. "I'm sorry, I'm overflowing. Excuse me, if you just give me a moment..."

"Please don't apologize, Ariana. It's something natural... and very provocative," he said hoarsely, now resting a hand on each of her knees.

She was the perfect height in that position, her chest directly in front of his face. His cock was so hard, being so close to his deepest, darkest fantasy.

Ariana thought that she heard him wrong and in a confused voice asked "Provocative?"

Now Lorenzo looked up and into her eyes. "You have no idea how tempting you are to me. You are a woman like no other, Ariana. You are so strong, independent, sweet, beautiful. If you were mine, I would remind you every day how special you are. How much I would like to take care of you and Irene, you wouldn't stay up at night worrying."

Ariana was dumbfounded by Lorenzo's unexpected confession. She had no idea that he felt that way about her. He had always been so courteous, so kind, but he had never hinted at anything that would reveal what he was saying right now.

"I don't know what to say Lorenzo."

"Don't worry, Ariana. I know that a young and beautiful woman like you would never be interested in an old man like me."

"Oh my God, Lorenzo, you're not old. How old are you? 50? 55?"

"49."

"That's not old."

"How old are you?"

"27."

"I'm nearly twice your age."

Ariana didn't say anything, but she was shaking her head. He could call himself old all he wanted, but the reality was that he looked distinguished. A mature man who cultivated his mind and body. His dark hair was tinged with gray, and he had fine lines around his eyes, but that only added to his attractiveness. Not to mention his body; he had broad shoulders and bigger biceps than her ex. Any woman would be lucky to be by his side, she thought. Except for me, after what happened with Francisco, I don't think I'll ever be able to trust a man again.

Lorenzo didn't think she would accept his confession, but since he had nothing else to lose, he said "Can I ask you a favor, Ariana?"

"Sure, whatever."

"If you want, we could consider it as a way to pay off your debt for the last three months. But make no mistake, I'm not charging you, but think of it as a way to have peace of mind, so that you can sleep better... If you want to, and by doing this, you would be fulfilling my biggest fantasy."

"You're not going to propose that I sleep with you, are you?" She asked suspiciously.

"No, not that, Ariana. Something more innocent, and at the same time more wicked than that."

She raised her eyebrow in confusion.

"Well, I've fantasized about it for a long time, and I've never been able to do it. You'll think I'm sick old man... But I have already told you how I feel about you, and the truth is that the worst that can happen now is that you just say no."

Now Ariana was curious, "What kind of fantasy?"

"I want to drink your milk. I want to know what it tastes like, what it feels like..."

Ariana's eyes widened, she would never have imagined that Lorenzo would say such a thing to her! Her first reaction was no! Absolutely not! But she said nothing, she just looked at him kneeling there in front of her, watching her with those cinnamon colored eyes. They had never been in such close proximity for so long before, and in that proximity she could smell the masculine scent of his cologne, and even though he was kneeling on the floor, he still looked imposing and masculine.

He was a good man, a generous man, and even though what he was asking of her was quite strange, she couldn't deny that it wasn't a difficult thing to do. They weren't going to have sex, he just wanted to drink milk from her breasts, something her daughter did every morning and every night, and that had no sexual connotation at all. As soon as Irene was born, it was a painful experience, but as the days went by, her body adjusted; and now, a little over a year later, the sensation of nursing compared to the sensation of sucking her thumb, there was no erotic sensation in it, at all. And if pleasing this man, who had been so generous to her, was a way of repaying her debt, then in truth, it was an offer she couldn't refuse.

When she made her decision, she didn't say anything to Lorenzo; she simply took off her shirt, revealing her two large round tits, the milk that was overflowing from her painted her nipples with tiny white droplets.

Lorenzo gasped in disbelief at what he was seeing, she was agreeing to his proposal, she was inviting him to suck those exquisite breasts.

Ariana's face revealed nothing, her expression was perfectly impassive as she sat across from him shirtless. He looked at her, waiting for some sign from her part; she barely nodded, hinting that he had permission to drink from her.

He licked his lips, gazing at her milky nipples. Slowly he leaned into her chest, licked a white drop with the tip of his tongue, savoring her sweet nectar for the first time. Then he wrapped his lips around her nipple and sucked. His cock throbbed between his legs as his mouth was flooded with her delicious milk. It was sweet and warm. He filled his mouth with her cream.

Ariana gasped when he sucked her tit. This didn't

feel at all like when she ordinarily breastfed. As soon as his tongue and lips made contact with her nipple, a delicious electric current pulsed throughout all her nerve endings, it was as if her nipple and her areole awakened to a previously unknown peak of sensation. The pleasure was undeniably erotic, absolutely sexual. Her clit was triggered in the blink of an eye. She felt her pussy becoming slick while he sucked the milk from her breast.

Lorenzo detached himself from her luscious breast and saw a trickle of milk from her other breast slide down the curve of her tit and down her belly. Ariana wasn't exaggerating when she said she was overflowing. He latched onto her other full, creamy tit and sucked. His hands had gone up her thighs, leaning on her lap while he knelt before her, sucking her delicious milk filled tits.

He was trying to control his desire; he wanted to rub against her body, caress every inch of her skin, squeeze her full bosom with his hands. He didn't want to scare her off, but he was caught in the whirlwind that assaulted his senses. The effort to separate himself from her creamy source was the most difficult thing he had ever had to do; he didn't want to stop.

As he stopped drinking from her, he looked at her face; but now Ariana's expression was not indifferent. Her lips were parted and she was panting softly, her pupils were dilated, her breasts rose and fell in time with her breathing. She was just as turned on as he was. And when she whispered "Don't stop, Lorenzo. Please, don't stop," her plea unleashed his lust. He grabbed her tits with both hands, clutched and squeezed her flesh, filled his mouth with her sweet milk and let it run down her chest, painting white streams on her skin while he suckled and milked her.

He pulled away from her far enough to press her tits together, he pinched her nipples, the fine sprays of white, creamy liquid raining down on his face.

He resumed drinking from her voraciously, and Ariana was now sitting further towards the edge of the chair, undulating her hips, unaware of the level of arousal that was taking over her. She tangled her fingers in his hair and arched her back, rubbing Lorenzo's face against her tits. He moaned as he drank from her and Ariana said, "I don't know what you're doing to me, Lorenzo, but it feels so good! I never wanted to be with someone else again, but now the only thing I want is to feel you inside me. I need you to fuck me!"

A possessive growl rumbled in his chest, he cradled her face in her hands and replied, "You have made me the happiest man in the world, Ariana," and he sealed her lips with a passionate kiss.

Their tongues intertwined, kissing, breathing frantically, hungry to devour each other.

Lorenzo took off his shirt and he stood up, he wrapped his arms around her waist and lifted her from the chair. Ariana circled him with her legs, their chests skin to skin. The softness of her breasts pressed against his chest made him shiver. With firm and sure steps, he went towards the master bedroom, carrying the woman whom he had fantasized about for so long. In her bedroom, he placed her on the bed and didn't stop kissing her.

He caressed her skin with his lips, Ariana writhing with hot desire. Her sex throbbed between her legs, begging to be filled.

Lorenzo finished undressing her and took a moment to contemplate her nakedness before burying his face between her legs. After drinking the sweet milk from her tits, the taste of her slick pussy exploded on his tongue, the contrasting flavors igniting his passion. He licked and sucked her folds with overwhelming hunger, he wanted to hear her moan and scream his name, he wanted to make her his in every possible way.

He reached underneath her body and gripped her ass, continuing to lick up and down her slit.

"Oh Lorenzo, I'm so close, you're going to make me cum!"

Even though he was dying to drink her orgasm with his mouth, he wanted her to cum their first time together with his cock buried deep inside her. He stopped licking her pussy and Ariana let out a frustrated groan; but when she saw that he was taking off the rest of his clothes, she felt a tremor of anticipation run through her body. It was so long since she had been with a man, more than a year of not feeling that undeniable desire to be rammed, that wild longing to be taken as if it were her last day on earth.

When he was completely naked in front of her, Ariana looked him up and down, appreciating his defined musculature, his strong, masculine figure. She was in awe of the size of his member, his hard cock rising between his legs, promising to impale and stretch her further than she had ever been.

Lorenzo knelt before her pink slit, glistening with her arousal, he slid the tip of his cock up and down her slit, spreading her folds and slowly penetrated her pussy.

Ariana gasped when she felt his bulbous head inside her, it had been so long...

"Tell me if you need me to stop."

"No, no, don't stop. I want you to fill me up."

Lorenzo penetrated her inch by inch until his balls rested against her ass. He was buried to the hilt, and the tight, moist heat from her channel was enough to push him over the edge in that instant.

He remained still inside her, giving her time to get used to the size of him; he groaned when she moved her hips, making his cock go in and out of her tight pussy.

Having this woman with her legs spread for him, taking his cock inside her, filled him with sensual joy. He leaned over her and kissed her before going back to drink the milk that continued to flow from her nipples, painting white rivulets on her skin.

Ariana again felt the electric current that went from her nipples directly to her clit. Her entire body was overstimulated, she raised her hips to meet his thrusts, getting closer and closer to the peak of ecstasy. He didn't stop suckling her tits, licking and drinking her cream; it felt like a decadent combination of making love while fucking her in the most perverse way he had ever experienced; and he never wanted it to stop. The orgasm built within her until it reached the point of no return, she moaned while wave after wave of pleasure shook her body and contracted every one of her muscles.

Her pussy sucked Lorenzo's cock with a desperate rhythm, as if she wanted to rip out his orgasm alongside hers. Lorenzo buried his face in her neck and thrust into her with brutal intensity as his balls contracted and his cock throbbed with each jet of cum that he emptied inside her.

Ariana moaned uninhibited, consumed by the sensation of his pulsing sex, releasing rope after rope of his sticky, hot cum that laced her channel.

She barely regained control of her senses when

Lorenzo wrapped his arms around her and lay down on her side without letting go.

"You have made me the happiest man in the world, Ariana. I only pray that this is not the only time that you give me the pleasure of your body and your company. I want you to be mine today and always. We will go as slow as you want, but ..."

Ariana turned her head and silenced him with a kiss.

"This has been the most unexpected and most incredible surprise that I have had with someone, Lorenzo. Of course I don't want this to be a one-time encounter. I want to do it so much I can't walk straight!" she giggled.

With those words, Lorenzo began to get hard again and said, "It will be my pleasure."

THE END

Creamy 4
and Overflowing
Naughty Cop
wants to Drink my Milk
Lesbian Lactation Erotica Short Story
Adriana Gala

Naughty Cop Wants to Drink my Milk

Creamy and Overflowing 4

It was almost 2:00 am when I got off work. I was driving home when I veered off the main road and looked for a quiet place to stop the car. My breasts felt like they were about to explode, I couldn't wait the 15 minutes it would take until I got home, I needed to express my milk now.

There was almost no traffic at that hour in the outskirts of town, but there were houses here and there that made their presence known by the porch lights that remained on.

I saw a clearing surrounded by trees less than a hundred yards away. The place looked nice and secluded, and the most important thing was that it was close.

The warm summer breeze blew in through the window as I reclined the seat and positioned my battery powered breast pump. I unbuttoned my work blouse and unhooked the front clasp of my bra. The breeze on my wet nipples made me shudder.

It had been hours since the last time I had pumped, and I felt an anticipatory tingle inside me at the prospect of expressing the creamy white liquid that was already dripping from my engorged breasts.

I changed the radio station until I found a song I liked and leaned back in the seat. I positioned the plastic shield on one of my hardened tits, around my enlarged nipple and turned on the portable machine. It made a humming noise as it clung to my chest and began to suck.

The first squirt of milk drew a pleased groan from my throat, it felt so good to release that excess pressure. Moments later my body began to respond to the stimulus of the machine and my milk flowed steadily, filling the container.

I can't deny it, when I pump my milk I become incredibly turned on. The violent suction of the machine over-stimulates my hypersensitive nipples. As the milk gushes from my tits, the moisture between my legs increases exponentially. It's almost impossible to resist the temptation to touch myself, and given the fortunate circumstances that I was alone in my car in the middle of the night with no one around, I wasn't going to waste the opportunity to play with myself a little bit.

I spread my legs and stroked my pussy over the elastic fabric of the short shorts that I had to wear at my waitressing job at Lola's, the most popular bar in town.

Since giving birth, my tits had gotten so big and voluptuous that the customers would stare at them mesmerized. Some even offered a very generous tip if I let them have a taste of my milk... straight from the source. It was tempting, part of me wanted to take more than a few patrons up on the offer. Knowing that all those guys wanted to suck my tits and drink my milk turned me on more than I wanted to admit; but I didn't want to get involved with someone who frequented my workplace. I need my job more than a wild night with promises of passion. So I would just turn to my trusty little machine to empty myself when necessary, and I'd touch myself when I got the chance, like tonight.

My slit was already slick with my juices when the machine began to pump, and each soft touch of my fingers on my pussy through the fabric of my shorts got me even more excited. I closed my eyes and imagined a man between my legs, his greedy mouth sucking on my big, milk-filled tits as his stiff cock filled my pussy. The fantasy had me squirming in the seat of my car.

"Oh my God!" I moaned into the silent night as I slipped my hand under the waist band and under my thong, my fingers finding my throbbing clit. I rubbed my clit faster and faster, slick and slippery from my juices. I was just about to cum when I was startled by a female voice. "Miss? Please turn on the light inside the car and place both hands on the steering wheel."

I heard the click of the flashlight as I quickly removed my hand from between my legs. With awkward movements I released the breast pump shield from my chest and turned it off.

"Yes, of course. One second, officer," I replied in a shaky voice.

I glanced in the rearview mirror and saw the police car in the rearview mirror me. I had been so absorbed in what I was doing that I didn't even realize she had parked right behind me.

I squeezed my eyes shut when the light from her

flashlight shone inside the car. I held the steering wheel tightly, trying to calm my hands that had started to tremble by the sudden interruption. The police officer leaned over and looked inside the car. Adrenaline pumped inside me, making my body flush.

It must have been obvious to her what I was doing, I was mortified. She was young and attractive, her uniform hugging her curves in all the right places. My body was still horny as hell; why didn't she arrive five minutes later? I felt my unsatisfied lust reverberating under my skin.

I am usually attracted to men, but I have had occasional flings with women; and there was definitely something about this cop that instantly appealed to me. She seemed irreverent and sure of herself, and her tits looked big and round under the dark fabric of her police uniform.

"Elsa Rodriguez," the officer read my name aloud from my driver's license, her eyes looking at the document and then at my face. "Do you live near here?" She asked, her face serious.

"Yes, officer," I replied with a nervous voice. I hadn't committed a crime or anything, but I felt anxious nonetheless; my heart was thumping in my chest. "I live about fifteen minutes from here."

"Then surely you know that this is not the safest place to park your car at this hour. Sometimes there are complaints from vagrants in the area, and there are overprotective owners with registered firearms who don't like to see strange cars parked around here."

"I know... it's just... I needed to stop for a moment," I stammered. My blouse was still unbuttoned and I could feel a thin stream of milk sliding down my belly. I couldn't move to clean it or button my blouse; I could only sit there under her disapproving gaze, my hands on the steering wheel.

"And why did you need to stop?"

I looked into her eyes and saw how her gaze drifted and saw the portable breast pump on the seat next to her. Her eyes twinkled and she understood. "Aaahh," she said with a half smile. "I see."

"It couldn't wait. I just got off work, but I needed to release the excess pressure, so I parked over here to pump."

My nipples were practically poking out of the vertical seams of my open shirt. I'm sure she had noticed, and I had no doubt that she could smell what I had been doing in addition to expressing my milk.

"Well, Miss Rodriguez," she said, taking out her ticket book. "I understand, but I still have to fine you."

"What!? But why!?" I asked indignantly. "I wasn't doing anything wrong!"

"Calm down, Miss. Exposing your breasts in a public place is lewd behavior, it carries a small fine."

"What the hell are you talking about? Do you see anyone around here? I'm here alone, in the dark, in my own car!"

"Hey!" She said with a commanding voice. "You can shut up and pay this fine or I can take you to the station for disrespecting a police officer!"

"Fuck you! I haven't been lewd or immoral, and you know it!"

"That's enough! Get out of the car Miss Rodriguez!"

"B ... b ... but ..." I stuttered as she opened the car door and pulled me out by my arm. I almost lost my balance on my heels, my boobs rocking and swaying inside my unbuttoned blouse, my nipples brushing against the fabric.

The cop made me walk to the front of the car and shoved me against the hood, crushing my breasts under my own weight as she placed handcuffs around my wrists.

Her body pressed against my back, I felt the softness of her tits when she whispered in my ear "They really make you dress like sluts down there at Lola's." She straightened and began to frisk me.

"Yeah… I guess," I said in a small voice, her hands exploring under my tits and around my waist.

It wasn't a lie, the shorts were very short, the blouses showed more than enough cleavage and were tied in a knot above our bellybutton, and the platform heels were pretty high. Although what she had said was true and she had me handcuffed against the hood of my car for no good reason, I knew that I should be furious; however, what I felt was heat radiating from my core and a hungry desire to appease the lust that I hadn't been able to satisfy.

The cop now ran her hands over my legs, patting my ass, brushing my sex, all under the argument that she was making sure I didn't have a concealed weapon.

"Are you arresting me?"

"No. I just have to check you and your car to make sure nothing illegal is going on."

I was still bent over the hood of the car, my boobs dripping onto the metal as the police officer looked inside again with her flashlight. Then I saw that she was holding something in her hand, it was the container with the milk that I had pumped.

"Mmmm, this looks delicious," she said. "I bet it's sweeter than a milkshake."

"Be careful with that!"

"Get up," she said authoritatively.

I obeyed and straightened my back, my white

blouse that still hung open was wet with my milk, making my blouse completely see through, my dark nipples protruding through the damp fabric.

"Do you still need to pump any extra milk?"

A chill ran through my body; the cop was ogling me, and I finally put two and two together. Oddly enough, I felt flattered and found myself wanting her, and wanting to find out what she really wanted to do with me.

"Yes, they're still very full," I whimpered.

The cop went back to the car window and took out the portable machine, the plastic shield still speckled with white drops.

"So it seems," she said almost like a purr, her hand brushing the side of my blouse, exposing my large, round breast. She brushed my skin and I shuddered with pent-up desire.

"Look at them, you're about to burst." Her finger tracing a path from one breast to the other, my blouse now fully open, exposing my swollen tits. My nipples wouldn't stop dripping.

The cop pinched one of my nipples and I felt like

an electric current traveled directly from my nipple to my clit, leaving me in a needy state. A fat white drop adorned the tip, it hung there precariously until it slid down the curve of my breast. Her attention was driving me crazy. "Please" I whispered, "I need to milk them."

The naughty cop gave me a mischievous smile, she placed the plastic shield on one of my tits and turned on the machine. I gasped when I felt the familiar pumping sensation.

"You like that, right?" She said as the breast pump sucked and spurted white cream from my chest. My breathing had quickened. I just nodded and threw back my head, enjoying as I much as I could in this strange and perverse situation.

My other nipple was dripping and dripping, begging to be sucked on as well. I wriggled, trying to loosen my hands cuffed behind my back. I arched my back, pushing out my chest as an offering, I couldn't bear it any longer.

"Please... please suck them." I begged.

The naughty cop turned off the pump and removed the plastic shield from my breast, she wore a victorious smile on her full lips. Then, she grabbed my breast and squeezed, causing a stream of milk to shoot out, painting her beautiful face white. She smiled again before wrapping her lips around it and sucked my overflowing cream. We both moaned. Her mouth felt wonderful. She began to massage my other breast with her hand, milking me, making the sweet liquid spray out in thin streams from my nipple before sucking on that one as well.

"Oh yes!" I groaned, "Please, keep doing that! Drink it all up."

The naughty cop noisily slurped and sucked my tits until the white liquid dripped from the corners of her mouth.

"I have never tasted anything so delicious," she said, wiping her mouth with the back of her hand and went back to suckling me.

Her hand then slid down to my pussy, the fabric of my thong and shorts was soaked with my arousal. Her hand rubbed my slit over my clothes, from front to back, I was on the verge of ecstasy, I wanted more, I needed more.

As if our longings were tuned in, the police officer pulled my shorts and panties down my thighs. "Come here, I want the whole meal". She sat me on the hood of the car and finished removing the clothes around my ankles. My thighs spread like a butterfly's wings, my wet sex anticipating her eager mouth.

"Look how wet you are! This is going to be like eating a delicious, juicy watermelon."

And just as she had wrapped her lips around my tits, now she devoured my pussy with her mouth, licking and sucking every inch of my slit.

Every stroke of her tongue made me shiver and moan. I wanted to touch her too, I wanted to squeeze her tits and touch her pussy, but I couldn't do anything with my hands cuffed behind my back. I could only sit back, open my legs and enjoy how this naughty cop was doing the most wicked and wonderful things to my body.

She brushed her hand over my folds, then buried two fingers into my slippery opening. Her other hand went up to my chest and squeezed one of my tits tightly, making my milk spill over like a fountain before licking the white cream from my skin.

After swallowing mouthfuls of my cream while she fingered my pussy, she said "Nothing like a mamacita's tits".

She groped and squeezed my breasts, milking me, making the creamy liquid spill from my nipples and run over my belly in white streams, sliding down to the valley of my sex, saturating me in the sweet, warm liquid that this naughty cop couldn't stop tasting.

She once again pressed her face between my legs, the scent of my milk and my arousal permeating the air around us. Her hands slid over my flesh bathed in white cream until her fingers parted my pink folds, revealing my throbbing clit. My clit was slippery with my milk and arousal, the cop licked her lips and looked into my eyes as she brought her mouth to my pussy and licked me like ice cream melting in the heat of the sun.

"Oh my God! Oh my God!" I whimpered, arching my back, pressing my pussy to her mouth and writhing on the hood of the car, desperate to rub myself on her face.

She covered my sex with her greedy mouth, she sucked, licked and lapped me up completely, inside and out, until I was panting and pleading "Don't stop! Don't stop! Don't stop!"

She expertly licked and teased my clit with her skillful tongue, kept pumping her fingers in and out of my pussy, making me body wind up as if she had tied me up with rope and then released me. The orgasm shook my muscles and a fountain of milk shot out of my nipples, the creamy jets spraying out of me to the beat of the waves of ecstasy that shook my body.

As the milk shot rhythmically out of my tits, the cop replaced her tongue with her thumb on my clit, rubbing my sex and covering one of my big nipples with her mouth. She sucked me hard and I felt another orgasm surge up and shake my body, her hand fucking me mercilessly as she alternated sucking on my tits, drinking my sweet milk in ravenous pulls.

I was spent, panting and spread eagled on the car. "God… that was amazing," I mumbled, drunk with pleasure.

I had never imagined how sensual and delicious it

would feel to have an orgasm being with someone while they sucked on my tits. I hadn't had sex with anyone since I found out I was pregnant, and now my baby was 10 months old. I knew that at some point I wanted to date again and have sex, but after this, I knew that it was something I would need, more than once.

My body vibrated in the wake of pleasure that this sexy and naughty cop had given me. I looked at her, I also wanted to touch her and make her cum; but before I could say anything, she said, "Well, Miss Rodriguez, this time I'll let you go with a warning."

She removed the handcuffs and hung them on her belt, leaving me to rub my sore wrists and get dressed. We had barely finished and I was already hungry for more.

"And next time?" I asked in a mischievous way.

The cop stopped and looked me up and down with a sexy smile.

"Next time," she said, stroking the length of the black baton that hung from her belt. "Next time I may be forced to use my nightstick on you. So I better not catch you here again. Understood?"

The phallic and smooth shape of her baton made my pussy clench with longing, I imagined how it would feel to have her fuck me with it while sucking on my milk-filled tits.

I nodded and said, "Got it, officer".

Without another word she turned and walked back to her patrol car.

THE END

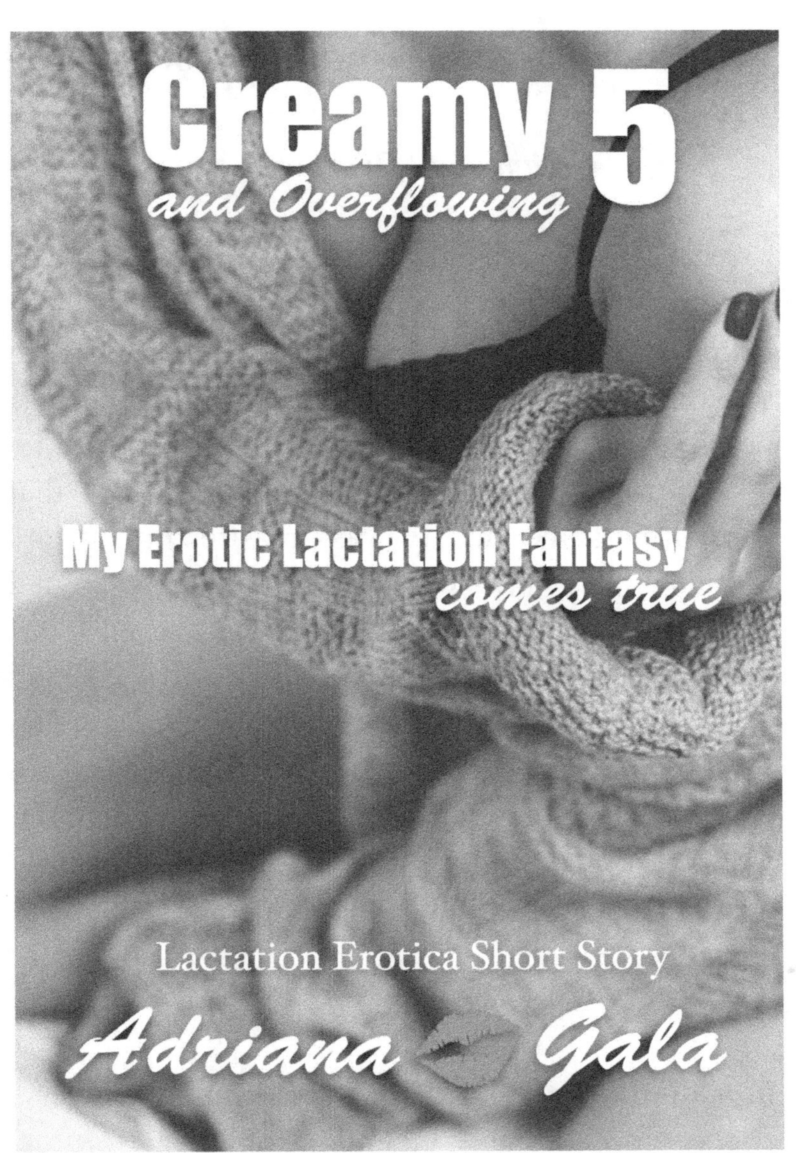

Creamy 5
and Overflowing
My Erotic Lactation Fantasy
comes true
Lactation Erotica Short Story
Adriana Gala

My Erotic Lactation Fantasy Comes True

Creamy and Overflowing 5

When I found out I was pregnant, I subscribed to several pages and blogs to learn as much as possible about this great new chapter in my life. Aside from the delivery, one of the things that caused me some anxiety was breastfeeding. Many friends, relatives, and even my own mother had told me that it was a painful ordeal; however, I was determined to breastfeed my baby. My husband was my rock throughout the pregnancy, he even went with me to a breastfeeding seminar; where we learned more in depth about the benefits it would provide for the new life growing in my womb, and the proper technique for the baby to breastfeed without causing the pain that so many women I knew complained about.

In addition to the seminar, I read all the articles I could find online, including various forums. Throughout my readings, I discovered that there were women who not only spoke of the joy of breastfeeding their child, but also that their husbands or partners drank the milk from their breasts. The idea intrigued me. At first I thought it was a bit strange, but the more I read about it, curiosity got the best of me. It's somewhat taboo, even though it really shouldn't be. It's a natural process in the body and quite an intimate connection. I could understand why so many couples did it.

After reading so many posts about numerous people who shared such a relationship, I found myself returning again and again to those forums, rereading all the messages, with an insatiable appetite to know more about it. I learned there is even a name for it, it's called adult breastfeeding or erotic lactation. I had no idea how my husband would react to it. What if he thought I was crazy or thought I had turned into a sexual pervert? I didn't want to gross him out if he thought it was unpleasant. I was becoming obsessed with the subject, but how could I share the idea with him? Did he have any idea that this existed?

The more and more I read about erotic lactation, the more turned on I became. I thought about it often, and fantasized about feeling my husband's lips wrap around my nipples and drink my milk when I touched myself in the shower. I would imagine that we were together watching television on the sofa, and that my blouse would get wet with the milk that spilled from my nipples; he would notice and gently caress my breasts over the fabric of my nightgown, pulling it down, exposing my moistened nipple and covering it with his mouth, sucking the white liquid and moaning with pleasure as he drank the milk from my tits. Just thinking about it got me aroused.

After the delivery and first six months, where my body healed and we got used to the changes that come with a baby, the idea of my husband sucking on my breasts consumed my thoughts when I thought of him sexually. I don't know why it turned me on so much; I hadn't even mentioned it, and it probably hadn't even crossed his mind.

I wondered how to tell my husband that I wanted him to drink my milk, but no matter how much I thought about it, I was too embarrassed to share my fantasies with him. I was terrified that he would reject me!

There were times when I teased him about tasting my milk, to see if I could figure out where he stood on that matter. But one night, before I gave birth, we were in bed together and he was fondling my breasts, which had already become twice their natural size. When he started sucking on my nipples, a bit of colostrum spurted out. Immediately he stopped and said, "Babe, I think your milk is starting to come in." After that night he never sucked my tits again. And now, months later, he ignored my breasts when we made love. I figured that making jokes about it would be an effective way to determine what he thought about the idea of drinking my milk; but he usually just chuckled and didn't say anything about it. I had no idea what he thought about this change in my body.

One night I stayed awake and sat in front of the computer trying to find out how other women posed the fantasy of erotic lactation to their husbands. No matter how many pages I visited, I didn't find the answer I was looking for, there were no stories online about couples broaching that topic. I felt deeply disappointed; I thought that my fantasy would never come true, and that after my baby finished breastfeeding I would never again have the opportunity to discover how it felt to have that sexual experience with my husband.

The next morning, I woke up and Julio was lying next to me, staring at me. I smiled sleepily at him and said, "Good morning". He replied the same and kept looking at me. "What are you doing?" I asked. "I love looking at you when you sleep. You look so beautiful". I smiled and closed my eyes again.

While we were lying in bed, I noticed that my back felt a bit sore, so I rolled over and asked him "Do you mind giving my back a rub? I'm feeling kind of achey". I groaned as his strong hands massaged my back, then he asked "What were you reading on the computer last night?"

I felt my heart skip a beat and I thought, 'Shit! Does he know? Did I remember to close the page I was reading?'

I answered in the most casual way I could, "Nothing in particular, just surfing the web."

"Were you reading about erotic lactation?"

Oh God! I couldn't believe I had been stupid enough not to close the page I had been reading. I was mortified, I wanted to disappear under the covers. What did he think of me now?

I took a deep breath and covered my face with one arm trying to hide my embarrassment. "Yes," I mumbled.

"Why were you reading about it?"

"Eeemm… I don't know. I guess because it was something I read mentioned in a forum."

"Is that something that interests you?" I mean, I just want to understand why you were reading about it.

Could this be more embarrassing? Here I was, totally mortified just thinking about how to mention this to him and here he was, chatting with me about my naughty fantasy that he discovered on the computer. Not only that, but he was talking to me about it just when I had woken up, I was completely unprepared. How did I respond? I didn't want to lie to him because I wanted to make my fantasy come true, but at the same time I didn't want him to think I was a pervert for thinking like that.

"I don't know," I said and pulled the blanket over my head.

He tried to pull the blanket away from my face, but I held it tight, letting him understand that I wanted it right where it was.

"Hey, it's okay. I just want to know what you're thinking."

"Can we not talk about this now?" I'm a bit embarrassed.

"Why? Are you ashamed? I just want to know if this is something you want to do with me?"

"Uummm… well… Yes… I didn't know how to talk to you about it before Juan Diego was born; when my milk started to come in and you tried it, you never touched or sucked my breasts again, so I assumed you didn't like it."

"That time it took me by surprise, that's all. But I didn't dislike it... not at all. But since you didn't say anything when I told you, I thought you didn't like the idea, so I left it at that. And while you were pregnant, and since Juan Diego was born… you look beautiful, and your breasts are so big. All I want to do is touch them, but I don't know if I'll hurt you or something."

Slowly I removed the blanket from my face and turned around, looking into his eyes I asked him "Really?"

He took the edge of the blanket and gently pulled it

further down, revealing my chest covered by a tank top that I had used to sleep. My nipples bulged against the fine fabric that covered me. I gasped when his hand slid up my belly and delicately touched one of my nipples through my tank top. The sensitivity in my nipples had grown exponentially, and my husband's caresses, although light, immediately sent waves of pleasure from my chest to my clit. It had been so long since he had touched my breasts, I never imagined that it would feel like this, that his touch would turn me on so quickly.

His hand went to my other nipple and traced the same delicate caresses, I could already feel the slickness making my panties wet. I closed my eyes, prey to the pleasure he was giving me, my breath quickening with every second he touched me.

"Do you like it?" he asked.

"Yes," I moaned. It felt so good, I didn't want him to stop.

I lay on my back and felt the heat of his body approach mine. Lying on his side, he leaned his thigh against mine and pulled my top down, exposing my breasts. When his lips wrapped around my nipple and sucked I thought I would cum right then and there. There was a reason they called it erotic lactation; I had never felt so turned on as I was now, it was nothing like when I was feeding my son. But here in bed, just the two of us, my husband squeezing one breast with his hand while sipping the milk from my other breast, it was a thousand times better than all those times I had masturbated fantasizing precisely about this type of encounter.

The tingling in my nipples and the throbbing, hungry sensation of my sex clouded my thoughts, I could only feel what my husband was doing to me.

He continued to suck on my tits, one and then the other, occasionally stopping to tease them with the tip of his tongue, his teeth brushing my taut peaks. When he licked my areola and sucked on my nipple, he looked up, looked at me, and smiled. God! I felt so good! I could see white droplets of milk at the corner of his lips.

The hand that was massaging one of my tits caused milk to flow from my nipple and slide down the curve of my breast, painting my skin with fine streams of sweet nectar. Seeing the white liquid, he uncovered me completely and finished undressing us. When he positioned himself between my legs, I could feel the warmth and firmness of his erection pressing against my sex; he traced my opening with his fingers, delving into my pink folds.

"You're so wet," he murmured against my lips before kissing me and penetrating my slit with his fingers.

I moved my hips, desperately wanting him inside me, I wanted him to fill me with his cock, I longed to feel his erection opening me up and filling me to the brim.

"Please, I want to feel you inside me" I begged.

"Not yet," he replied and I felt his body move, now his head between my legs.

He licked my pussy from one end to the other, lapping up the juices of my arousal when moments ago he was drinking the milk from my tits. I felt his tongue delving between my folds until he reached my clit. A strangled moan escaped my lips and I held his head with both hands as he furiously licked my throbbing clit. When she plunged two fingers into my soaked pussy, an overwhelming orgasm erupted from my core, making me tremble all over. His mouth was fused with my sex, despite my convulsions of pleasure he didn't stop devouring me, licking and sucking my clit voraciously. When my body started coming down from that incredible high, he gave me no chance to recover, he knelt between my legs and pushed his hard cock inside me, stretching me with his thickness.

He leaned over and his mouth returned to my tits, drinking the creamy milk that flowed from my nipples. I was overcome, it was pure sensation, to feel him taking me with such desire, my legs hugging his waist as he moved in and out of my channel, my fingers tangled in his hair as he suckled one breast, then the other, the evidence of my milk painting his lips white.

Another orgasm was growing inside me, and with each thrust of his cock the rhythm quickened, I was so turned on, and hearing his growls of pleasure dissolved me in pure lust.

I squeezed him with my inner muscles and gasped, "You're going to make me cum again, love."

"And you're about to make me cum," he replied.

His rhythm became brutal, both his hands held on to my tits and started to squeeze them, milking me, making me spray white threads of cream from my nipples.

You are mine, only mine

"Do you like it when I drink your milk?" he asked while he brutally fucked me.

"Yes! I love it! It feels so good when you drink the milk from my tits! It turns me on so much!" I moaned.

"I love your big, beautiful, creamy tits. I'm going to suck and squeeze them whenever I can."

"Yes! Yes! Yes!"

As my sex contracted around him with my second climax, I felt his cock pulse inside me as he shot rope after rope of his hot cum deep in my womb, claiming me as his wife.

My hands squeezed his arms, I could feel all his muscles tense while he came, his pleasure in sync with mine.

We remained fused, our bodies embraced as we

panted. Without a doubt, the connection between us had risen to a level that I wouldn't know how to explain; I was more than satisfied to have made my fantasy come true, unable to imagine the intense and exciting encounters that lay ahead.

THE END

Creamy 6
and Overflowing
Thirsty Client
in the Board Room
Lactation Erotica Short Story
Adriana Gala

Thirsty Client in the Board Room

Creamy and Overflowing 6

If I didn't move now, I would be late for the big meeting we had scheduled for this afternoon. This was just what I needed! I should have expressed my milk during my lunch break, but I put it off by sitting at my desk tweaking details in my presentation that didn't really need any changes. My perfectionism was costing me the comfort in my own skin. I felt like my breasts weighed more than two bricks.

My baby had been born 10 months ago, and I was lucky that my mother could take care of him while I worked as a Marketing Analyst. I had been working over a month to perfect the presentation that we would make today to Victor Castillo, CEO of the largest supermarket chain in the country. If I got this contract for the company, it would be the best thing of my professional career.

Making sure my clothes were spotless, I grabbed my bag with the USB stick that contained my presentation and headed for the board room.

I waited for everyone to sit down and began the presentation. Charlie, one of the members of the creative team, made sure that each part of the presentation appeared according to what I was saying. To my left were three of the most important men in the company, the Managing Director, the Marketing Director, and Chief Financial Officer. To my right was Victor Castillo, our potential client.

I had explained most of the strategy that we intended for the client, I was going over the final details, feeling triumphant, certain he would sign with us.

"We need to reach the younger clientele," I managed to say through gritted teeth as sharp pain shot through my chest.

"The SuperMax chain needs to adapt its message in order to appeal to people between 18 and 35 years old," I exhaled and grimaced.

"Are you alright, Marian?" The Marketing Director asked with a frown.

I smiled kindly at the men around me.

"Where was I? Oh! Right! For the SuperMax chain

to appeal to this group, it's important that they show where their produce comes from; healthy foods are what people are focused on now," I say and suddenly two buttons on my blouse popped.

A half smile raises the corner of Victor's lips while the rest of the men in the board room look at me in horror.

I make the closing statement, and as if things couldn't be more awkward, another button succumbs to the inevitable swelling of my breasts. At that moment, part of my bra is already visible through the unexpected opening of my blouse.

I cross my arms over my chest, trying to hide my wardrobe malfunction; however, I don't think I can hide the blush on my cheeks in such an embarrassing situation.

Victor is smiling from ear to ear and gets up from his seat. After looking me up and down he turns to the Managing Director, "I see what you're trying to do, John."

The man simply rolls his eyes and responds, "I have no idea what you mean."

"Your team has definitely tried their hardest,"

Victor says, his eyes on me again.

The Managing Director laughs nervously, and I am still there, standing like a statue with my arms crossed over my chest, wishing the ground to open under my feet, because the impossible to ignore pain in my breasts has expanded to the point of desperate need for relief, which meant that milk was already leaking from nipples, which was consequently wetting the fabric of my bra and my blouse.

Victor looks at me with his dark eyes and says "Can I talk privately with...? What is your name again?"

I open my mouth to answer but the Marketing Director speaks for me, "Marian, her name is Marian."

"Exactly... Marian."

The Managing Director looks at me and shrugs, gestures for the rest to leave the board room, leaving me alone with the client.

In a few steps he is standing in front of me.

"I'm sorry for what happened," I apologize.

"I'm not complaining," he says and I feel like he's undressing me with his eyes. "You certainly are a part of the new demographic that your marketing strategy suggests that my company adopt, am I right?"

"I suppose you're right, I'm a young, single working mother; I'm always interested in meals that are healthy and easy to prepare."

"So you could be in charge on handling this account, and work with me side by side, to implement and ensure that the new marketing strategy is effective?"

"Well... yes. If you decide to sign with us, the company would provide the necessary personnel to handle the account," I replied, wishing that this commanding man would choose our advertising company.

"But I don't want just anybody to be in charge of my account, I want it to be you," he said, looking at me intensely as his hands surrounded my waist and pulled me towards him.

My heart skipped a beat, I didn't understand what was happening. It had been a long time since any man had found me attractive; but apparently Mr. Castillo thought otherwise.

I moved my arms and rested my palms on his chest, which felt muscled under his shirt and jacket.

"Um… this is unprofessional, Mr. Castillo."

"Call me Victor."

"Alright, Victor. I don't think we should do this."

"Why not? I think you could use a little release. You seem somewhat... overloaded," he said looking at my chest.

I followed his gaze and let out an embarrassed groan. I had stopped covering myself, so the wet stains on my blouse were completely obvious. I tried to cover myself again, but Victor was faster than me and his big hands grabbed my wrists.

Before I could wallow any more in the shame I was feeling, Victor was kissing me, his lips on mine, his tongue parting my mouth. It took me a second to react, but my body was more alert than my mind, because I was responding to that kiss with the same intensity.

He released my hands and started to unbutton my blouse. He stared at my engorged breasts that threatened to pop out of my bra before turning me and lifting me with his strong arms to sit me on the polished surface of the conference table. The soft fabric of my bra was soaked through from the milk dripping from my full breasts. He slid the straps down my shoulders and pulled down the soggy material, my dark nipples exposed to the cold air in the board room. The constant drip slid in a thin stream of milk from each of my nipples, painting white rivulets down the curve of my breasts.

"Beautiful," he gasped before squeezing them together, an act that triggered an involuntary "Ouch!" from my lips.

He took hold of his excitement and stopped squeezing them so intensely. "I'm so sorry, Marian. I'll be more careful," and without giving me time to respond, he leaned toward my chest and ran his tongue over the tip of my nipple. He licked, over and over again, delicately drinking the milk that dripped from one nipple and then the other. Every time I felt him licking my sensitive peaks, it was as if an electrical current expanded within my core. When he wrapped his lips around my nipple and sucked, the pleasure was overwhelming. I was so aroused I couldn't think anymore, I just wanted to feel his wicked mouth sucking on my tits, drinking my milk.

"Mmmm, delicious," he murmured when his lips turned to suck my other tit. As he suckles, I can feel the jets of milk filling his mouth. He sucks and sucks, emptying my breasts, leaving them soft and pliable when before they were hard and aching.

I am so turned on that I am willing to do anything this man asks of me, so when he starts to take off my clothes, I help him undress me.

I am clouded with desire, ignoring the fact that my bosses and the rest of my colleagues are outside of the board room. I'm letting myself be seduced by the client, I'm letting this unknown man do whatever he wants with me because his daring appetites have left me like a cat in heat.

I am only wearing my heels, I am completely naked on the conference table and I spread my legs wantonly. He wastes no time, and in seconds he pulls out his erection, positions his hard and swollen cock in front of my wet pussy and pushes into me. His thickness feels so good inside me, stretching me to accommodate him; he makes me feel more feminine than ever as he fucks me on the table in the board room and sucks my tits again.

His length pumps in and out of my channel, his shaft coated with my juices, while his mouth greedily drinks the milk from my tits. He nurses from one and his hand pinches my other nipple, milking me, pulling a thread of the sweet whitish liquid that he wants so much.

The sound of our bodies colliding while he fucks me has an erotic and perverse rhythm that only turns me on even more. I grab his head and press it against the tit he's sucking, "Don't stop, don't stop" I moan in pleasure, "Keep sucking them just like that, drink all of Mommy's milk!"

I feel him growl with pleasure and suck even harder, my moans becoming louder and louder. I no longer care if they can hear us out there, I just want to feel Victor's hard cock thrusting between my legs and his mouth sucking on my tits, drinking the creamy milk that flows from my nipples and filling his mouth with its sweet taste.

Then I feel the absence of his mouth, I want to complain, but his lips on mine silence what I was going to say. The taste of my milk permeates his breath, further increasing this desperate arousal that consumes me.

His hands fondle and massage my tits, now soft but not empty. He breaks the kiss and looks at me before him, wide open and at his mercy, his thick cock moving in and out of my hungry pussy. He squeezes my tits and the white liquid drips from my nipples, threads of milk painting my abdomen, bathing the triangle of my sex.

I am so close that I can feel the orgasm threatening to explode inside me; I can't take it anymore and I put my hand between my legs, I rub my swollen clit, which is slippery with my milk and the juices from my pussy, I rub myself faster and harder. I can't take it anymore, the orgasm consumes me completely, I open my mouth in a silent cry of pleasure as the climax vibrates through my body, pulsing from my clit and causing my tits to spray milk like a fountain.

I move my hips, possessed by the bliss that this man is making me feel, my pussy squeezes down on his swollen cock, clenching around his thickness. I mistakenly think that he is also about to cum, but he's not. When my body stops shaking, he pulls his cock out of me only to flip me over on the table. I moan when I feel the loud slap on my ass, despite having had the most intense orgasm of my life, and even though my legs are still trembling, I am still so aroused.

I gasp when I feel him thrust into me from behind, filling my pussy with his hard cock. What had begun with delicate licks and soft caresses, is now replaced by savage carnal instinct. I arch my back, lifting my ass even higher as it slaps against his hard body while he fucks me. His hands venture up my waist and lifts my chest off the table, the focus of his fingers on touching, squeezing, and pinching my tits.

In front of us is the dark monitor of the flat screen TV of the board room, which serves as a perfect mirror. I can see the wild pleasure on Victor's face as he fucks me, his cock pumping in and out of my slippery pussy again and again. My face also wears the same expression of sensual desire, I feel like the hottest woman in the world with this man fucking me hard and fast while he milks my tits, already small puddles of milk forming on the polished surface under my breasts.

The way he pinches my nipples feels like he's touching directly between my legs, I can't believe this man is going to make me cum again. A strangled moan comes out of my throat as I feel another orgasm explode from my core and ripple under my skin like wildfire. My body trembles with each contraction of my climax, there is still milk in my tits and I watch in wonder how the last threads of milk shoot out of my nipples.

I'm exhausted with pleasure, I lean my torso on the table, my muscles shaking, but Victor isn't done yet. He thrusts his hard cock between my legs a few more times before pulling out.

"Now daddy has something for you," he says with his cock in his hand. "Is mommy ready to drink all the cum I have for you?" he continues as I stand up and turn to him.

I kneel before the client, a man who has given me the naughtiest sexual pleasure in my entire life, eager to please him in. I open my lips and let him put his cock in my mouth, it tastes like me, and makes me feel deliciously wicked. My tongue licks around his swollen shaft and bulbous head as he pushes in and out of my mouth. Then his length pushes in as deep as he can to the back of my throat. My lips stretch around his thickness as I noisily suck his cock, enjoying how he fucks my face.

I hear his guttural moan the moment his cock swells in my mouth, then the first jet of his sticky cum lands on my tongue. He is consumed with pleasure as he shoots rope after rope of his white cum in my mouth and it slides down my throat. I drink his salty cum with perverse pleasure like when he drank my sweet milk.

Satiated by our naughty encounter, it takes us about ten minutes to look decent again. Fortunately, I had everything I needed in my bag to look civilized after that incredible fuck.

"Consider it a done deal, Marian. I look forward to continuing to work with you... side by side," Victor says with a smile. He kisses me and leaves the board room.

I sit down, my head still spinning from everything that happened this afternoon. I pull another tissue out of my bag and finish wiping up the milk that had spilled on the conference table when the door opens and the Marketing Director walks in with a big smile on his face.

"Excellent work, Marian! I don't know how you

convinced him, but Victor is in John's office right now signing the contract; and he has specifically requested that you be in charge of the account."

I smile and nod at the Marketing Director, the taste of the client's cum still lingering on my tongue.

THE END

Creamy 7
and Overflowing
I Cheated on my Husband
with Two Delivery Guys
Adriana Gala
Lactation Erotica Short Story

I Cheated on my Husband
with Two Delivery Guys

Creamy and Overflowing 7

Have any of you ever been with a man who is selfish in bed? I assure you, it is beyond frustrating.

Last week my husband and I were in bed, ready to go to sleep when he hugged me from behind and began to slide his hands over my hips and waist with suggestive caresses. I turned around and he kissed me deeply, pulling my body towards his; not even two minutes had gone by when he told me, "Come on baby, suck my dick. You give such good head."

I guess I'm what you call a people pleaser, so I knelt on the bed with my face between his legs and sucked my husband's dick. Do you know what he did for me? The only moment he touched me was when we started kissing in bed, because the only thing he did while I sucked him off was hold my head while I went down on him. He didn't even grab my ass, or finger me. Not even my tits! Although, to be honest, he hasn't paid my breasts any attention since I gave birth, and that was 2 years ago! And when he was close, he pulled himself out of my mouth and fucked me doggy-style until he came.

Up until I got pregnant, he always wanted to touch my body. Once when I was washing the dishes, he came up behind me and put his arms around me, he started to squeeze my breasts and then reached under my skirt, slid my thong to the side and penetrated my slit with his finger, while he pushed his finger in and out of my pussy, he rubbed my clit with the other hand. He made me cum, right there, standing in the kitchen, just touching me. But nowadays, he just wants me to suck his dick, let him fuck me, and go to sleep, he doesn't care if I have an orgasm or not.

It was a typical Wednesday morning the day after that particularly frustrating encounter, my husband had already left for the office and I had dropped my toddler off at daycare. That day I was expecting the delivery of a new bed we had bought, so I was waiting for the delivery guys to bring it over and put it together in my bedroom.

When I opened the door for them, I was dressed casually in skinny jeans and a tank top that showed off my cleavage. Both guys stared at my chest before forcing themselves to look at my face. I smiled and invited them in, feeling happy that at least someone admired my looks, especially by these two men. I had to keep reminding myself to stop staring at them; they were two very handsome young guys, and each chance I got I'd check them out, their shirts stretched across their broad backs and hugged their strong biceps. They were undeniably hot, both their bodies looking so strong and muscular, surely a consequence from their manual labor.

They unloaded the boxes from their truck and I guided them to my bedroom, where I needed them to take the old bed apart and assemble the new one. I was fascinated watching them work, here I had two big, burly men working with a drill and hammer, disassembling my old bed and putting together the new one in such a methodical and synchronized way that the attraction I felt towards them only increased.

After they put the mattress on the new bed frame I brought them some coffee and cookies on a tray. The were both genuinely astonished and grateful for the gesture, making comments that some places they went to didn't even offer them a glass of water.

To that I replied "Well that's just plain rude, there are too many people that seem to have been raised without any manners. It doesn't matter if you're in a mansion or a hut, good manners are the true face of class and education. My grandfather always said 'Lo cortés no quita lo valiente', which means that by being courteous you're no less brave."

Sam and Bobby smiled at me, then Sam said, "Too bad you're already married ma'am, because you're one in a million. If you were single, I'd ask you out."

I tried to be graceful and smile, but I'm sure what came out was a grimace. They both noticed it, but it was Bobby who dared to ask, "Problems in paradise?"

I just shrugged my shoulders, but the truth is that I felt unhappy and frustrated, so confessing my marital problems to two strangers whom I might never see again seemed like a suitable way to unburden myself.

"It's something that I'm sure just happens to all marriages over time... but I think my husband doesn't find me attractive anymore. I'm the dutiful wife, but I'm not a woman he desires anymore."

"Well, with all due respect ma'am, but your husband must be blind! If I were him, not a day would go by where you weren't cherished, and know that you are definitely the most beautiful woman to walk the face of the earth!"

Bobby's compliment made me blush, but I have to confess that what he said made me feel a lot better.

They had finished the coffee and cookies I had brought them, but they stood rooted to the spot, like they didn't want to leave; and to be honest... I didn't want them to go either. Their company and chatter had lifted my spirits, and the way their eyes roamed my body was something I hadn't felt in a long time, and I liked it.

I missed feeling wanted, and these men were letting me know that they thought I was desirable.

I crossed my arms over my chest, unsure of what to do now; and by doing this I crushed my breasts together, making them more noticeable. Sam licked his lips, and Bobby's eyes were glued to my cleavage; he again dared to voice his thoughts, the sexual tension that was growing between these two strangers and I in the bedroom I shared with my husband was palpable.

"You're one of the most beautiful women I have ever seen. You're nice, kind, and very sexy. Forgive me, but your husband is a fool if he's not making you feel like a queen each and every day."

I bit my lip, I couldn't believe what I was going to do, but I desperately wanted what Bobby was saying, I wanted to feel like a queen, a goddess worthy of worship. So I said, "And how would you make me feel like a queen?"

Sam took advantage of that moment to highlight his presence and said "If you want, we can show you how a woman like you should be treated every day of her life."

I looked at each of these imposing males in the eye; desire, nerves, and anticipation were a rampant whirlwind inside me, I barely whispered "Okay". And the two men moved in unison, with that synchronized manner as when they were working on my new bed.

Sam wrapped his arms around my waist and kissed me; his tongue slid into my mouth and I found myself passionately kissing him back.

Bobby came up behind me, I could feel his erection pressing against my ass while his hands went to my breasts. He started squeezing my tits, pinching my nipples, I don't remember the last time I had ever felt so aroused. My breasts were hypersensitive. Ever since I had started breastfeeding two years ago, my nipples had become highly sensitized; and whenever I masturbated, I had taken to fondling my breasts, sucking my own milk covered fingers and using the sweet liquid to rub over my clit.

I worried thought popped into my mind: What if Sam and Bobby wanted to stop what we were doing as soon as the saw my milk dripping? I didn't breastfeed my son as often now as when he was an infant. I was certainly a bit full. Before I could say anything, Sam lifted me in his arms and placed me gently on the bed. He pulled my tank top over my head, and took off my bra while Bobby unbuttoned my jeans and dragged them down my thighs along with my thong, leaving me completely naked before them.

"My God, you're perfect," said Sam, at the same time as Bobby said, "You are too hot."

Their compliments made my head rush, they were making me feel utterly feminine and sexy. I didn't want this to stop.

Sam pressed his lips against mine again, a moan escaping my throat when I felt Bobby's wet tongue separating my folds. I didn't even remember when was the last time my husband had gone down on me, even though he always asked me to do it to him; and now I was naked, breaking in our new bed with the two delivery guys.

Bobby's tongue was buried in my slit, licking the slickness of my arousal. He murmured, "God, you taste so good."

Sam trailed kisses down my neck, his hands were groping and squeezing my breasts. His lips wrapped around one of my nipples and sucked. His sucking triggered my let-down reflex, and suddenly my milk started to flow.

"What?!" he said confused, looking down at both my tits and identifying the taste of my milk in his mouth.

I felt myself blushing from head to toe.

"I... I'm sorry. I should've told you... I'm still lactating... If you want to stop... I get it" I said ashamed.

"Stop? Why? Good God, woman! This makes you even sexier!"

Bobby looked up from between my legs, curious as to what was happening.

"Dude, you gotta get over here and suck on her big, luscious titties. Diana here is a Milky Milf."

"I'm a Milf?" I asked, flattered and astonished by the compliment.

"Hell yeah! You're one hot mama. And I want to drink up all your sweet milk."

Suddenly I had one man sucking on each breast, licking up my overflowing cream. It felt like heaven. I arched my back, pushing up my breasts, loving their tongues and mouth that were licking and nursing from me.

After Bobby seemed to have his fill from my breast, he went back down to my pussy, licking my clit with his deft tongue. Pleasure from the attention of both men washed over me. Bobby penetrated my wet slit with one finger, fucking my pussy with his hand while he sucked and licked my throbbing clit, and Sam alternated sucking on my breasts, greedily drinking my milk. The pleasure was overwhelming; my body shook with the orgasm that radiated through my body.

But when I was coming down from my climax, Bobby didn't stop, he kept licking my pussy, drinking my juices like a man dying of thirst who finally found a spring of water. I groaned as another orgasm overtook me; my pussy clenched around his fingers, my back arching and fine jets of milk sprayed from my tits, drops of milk on Sam's face, my chest and stomach. Even after my second orgasm, Bobby kept licking, sucking, kissing my sex, until I couldn't take it anymore and begged for mercy.

I was panting, my skin electrified, every cell in my body awake; and while I lay exhausted on the bed, Bobby pulled his face out from between my legs, his lips and chin covered with my juices, he said, "Your pussy tastes so good I could eat you out all day. But I'm so hard now I just need to put my cock in you."

I felt Bobby's large, swollen member pressing against my entrance. I could only moan when his hard cock rammed me. He was much bigger than my husband, but he had made me so wet with his saliva and my own arousal that I was able to take him, my pussy stretching around his fat cock.

Bobby practically growled with pleasure.

"You're so tight and wet, hot mama. This is the finest woman I've ever had, right, bro?

Sam filled his mouth with milk from my breast and kissed me, pushing the sweet liquid from his mouth to mine in the most erotic and wicked kiss I'd ever had. I drank my own milk from his mouth and he replied to his friend, "This woman is an angel fallen from heaven, bro." Without taking his eyes off me he said, "You're a goddess, hot mama!"

I looked into his dark eyes and found his erection with my hand, wrapping my fingers around his hard cock.

"You got me rock hard, hot mama" and he kissed me again.

"I want your cock in my mouth."

Bobby then pulled out of my pussy, and as if I weighed no more than a feather, my two strong lovers flipped me over on the bed, putting me on my hands and knees; Bobby thrust his cock back into me from behind and in front of my face was Sam's hard cock. I wrapped my lips around his smooth head and sucked him better than I had ever sucked my husband's dick. His big veiny member filled my mouth, while Bobby's length filled my pussy. Sam groaned as my tongue licked up his shaft and I sucked on his head, then swallowed the length of him deep to the back of my throat.

While I sucked Sam's cock, I turned my head a little and saw our reflection in the mirror. Just looking how these two men were pounding into me on both ends had me moaning, and as soon as Bobby started rubbing my clit I came. My body writhing in pleasure, desperately laving Sam's cock with my tongue and pushing back my ass onto Bobby's fat cock.

Bobby was ramming me harder and harder until I felt his cock swell inside me.

"I'm gonna cum, hot mama. I'm gonna fill your pussy with my cum."

When Bobby pulled out of my body, I felt his hot, sticky cum pour out of my slit and run down the inner part of my thighs. As if on cue, Sam pulled his cock from my mouth and sat on the bed. He pulled me onto his lap and I impaled myself on his cock.

He grabbed my ass and pushed me up and down his shaft with his strong arms, burying his fat cock in my pussy that was dripping with his friend's cum. His mouth found one of my nipples and he sucked hard, coaxing more milk from my tits.

He buried himself to the hilt, over and over again, bouncing me on his cock, and sucking my tits. It felt so good and naughty at the same time. Once again the pleasure built up within my core and I dug my fingers into his shoulders, holding onto him as I came all over his cock. As soon as my muscles clenched around him and the fine jets of my milk squirted onto his tongue and down his throat, I felt his cock swell inside me. He sucked my nipple hard while he came, rope after rope of his thick cum filling my womb.

"You're amazing, hot mama." He said before kissing me.

This has been, without a doubt, the hottest sexual experience of my life. It was wicked and dirty, but at the same time sweet and empowering, I loved it! And after saying goodbye to the two strong delivery men who made me feel like the most beautiful woman in the world, I didn't even shower or anything. I spent the rest of the day feeling how their cum drenched my panties.

THE END

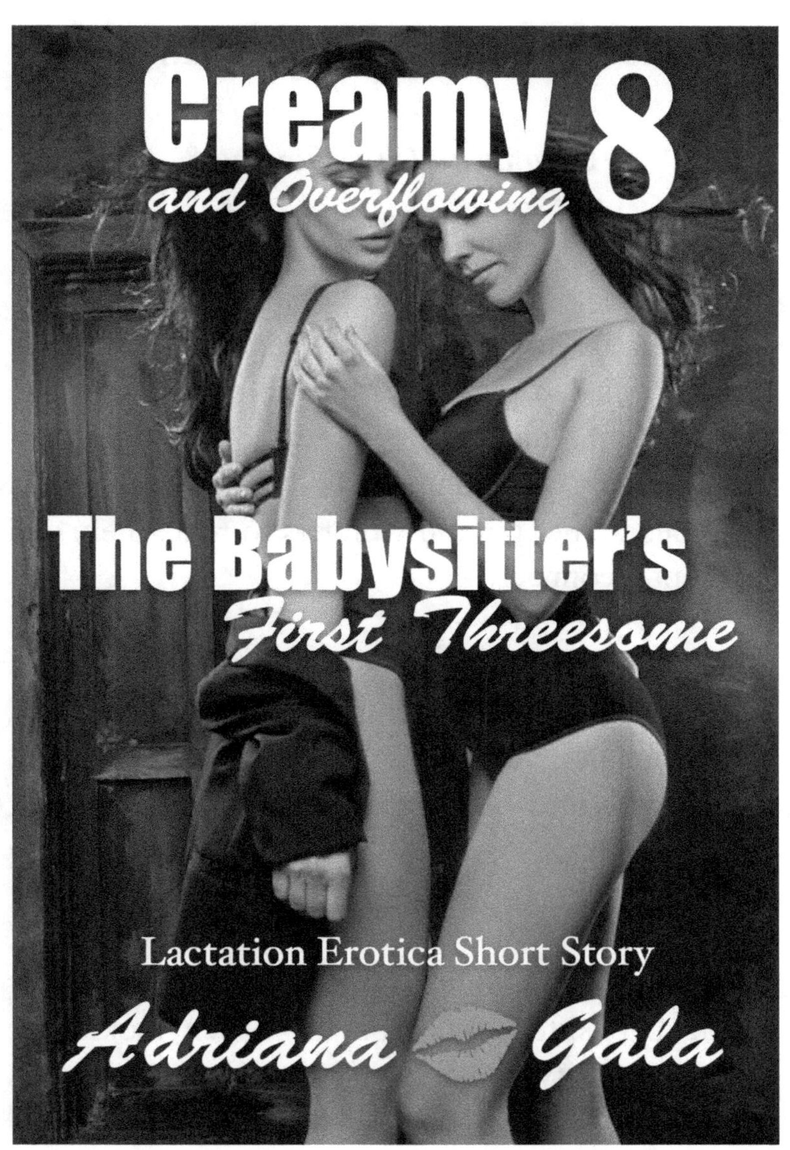

Creamy 8
and Overflowing
The Babysitter's
First Threesome
Lactation Erotica Short Story
Adriana Gala

The Babysitter's First Threesome

Creamy and Overflowing 8

It was almost midnight when Laura and Chris got home. It had been more than three weeks since they had a night just for the two of them without the kids, and an evening with a good movie and delicious dinner out did wonders to relax them and let them reconnect.

As Laura opened the door, she went in first and Chris didn't resist the temptation to grab her ass, squeezing her voluptuous flesh, already eager to take his wife to bed. He was harder than a rock, since she hadn't stopped stroking his throbbing erection as they drove home.

As they walked into the living room, they saw their young babysitter sitting on the couch looking at her phone. Katy looked up and smiled at them.

"How was your date?"

"It was great," Laura answered, sitting on the back of the sofa while Chris went to check on the little ones, who were sound asleep. "What about your night? Have the boys given you a lot of work?"

"Not at all," she said, waving her hand. "Your boys are fun, and they behave really well. They've been asleep for a while now."

"Thanks, Katy. You're the best! I don't know what we would do without you when Chris and I want to treat ourselves and go out on a Saturday. Surely your boyfriend must be angry that we kidnapped you tonight."

With that last sentence, Katy's cheerful countenance darkened.

"What happened, dear? Did you and Ben have a fight?"

"We broke up" she answered, squeezing her eyes shut to stop herself from crying.

Laura quickly sat down next to her and gave the young girl a comforting hug.

"It's going to be ok, hun. Don't be sad, you'll find someone better in no time."

Katy broke away from the hug and said, "I'm no

sad, Laura, I'm angry!"

"What did he do?"

"That idiot has been cheating on me!"

"What!? With who?"

"You mean with how many..." Katy replied bitterly.

Laura raised her eyebrows in amazement.

"And now I feel furious because I think I should have done the same to him before I broke up with him! You have no idea how angry I am!!"

"Believe me, I can imagine how you feel. There is no woman on earth who hasn't been betrayed in one way or another."

Katy looked at her with an expression of disbelief. Laura was 15 years older than her, but she took great care of herself. Even after having two children, she had a curvy and sexy figure. She had big breasts, which she would give anything to have compared to her medium-sized bust. And the way she talked and acted with such confidence, Katy only hoped that she would have that attitude when she was her age. She couldn't imagine that anyone would cheat on Laura, she was amazing.

"I don't believe you," Katy said. "You are way too beautiful, Laura! Who would cheat on you?"

Laura laughed, she felt flattered and reached out to affectionately caress her cheek.

"I think the same of you, Katy. Ben doesn't know what he's lost."

Katy smiled gratefully at the compliment and then shrugged.

"At least I didn't let him fuck my ass ..."

As soon as the words were out she put a hand over her mouth, mentally scolding herself at expressing herself like this. She was talking to the woman who paid her to take care of her children, not her girlfriends. Surely she would never want her to look after her kids again.

But instead of being offended by that comment, Laura laughed out loud.

She loved talking to this girl, she reminded her so much of herself when she was 20 years old. She felt an intense and protective affection for Katy, and wanted to help her in whatever way she could to avoid all those bitter thoughts that could invade your mind when you're young, curious, and insecure, incredulous of all the potential that lived inside her.

"Well, there you have your revenge," Laura said when she stopped laughing. "Send him a picture of someone else fucking you in the ass."

Now it was Katy's turn to laugh. She had been worrying that they wouldn't hire her anymore, and instead Laura was giving her advice on how to get revenge on her ex.

"Laura!!"

"What!? You think just because I'm a mom and happily married I don't have a nasty side?"

"I never would have imagined..."

"Why do you think Chris and I are so happy? We have a marriage based on trust, honesty, communication, and great sex."

"Yeah?"

"Of course. And I know what you're thinking. At first it hurts when someone fucks you in the ass, but if he knows what he's doing, it gives you the most intense orgasm of your life!" she winked at the babysitter.

Katy bit her lip and squeezed her thighs, the conversation was turning her on, and she wanted more than anything to have someone by her side to be as happy as Laura and Chris were.

"I'd love to find someone to do that with. But the truth is that so far the experiences I have had are not like what you read in books or see in movies."

"Oh hun, I'm sorry to hear that. You deserve to have the kind of sex that is so good even the neighbors have a cigarette."

Katy put her hand to her mouth and giggled, until they were both laughing out loud on the couch.

Chris came in to the room with an amused smile and a bottle of wine.

He placed the glasses on the table and handed the bottle to his wife, who grabbed it and drank straight from the bottle. The unsuspecting babysitter simply accepted it when Laura offered it to her, and drank a sip, also from the bottle, imitating Laura; not knowing that it was a secret way the couple communicated.

After making sure that the kids were sound asleep, Chris paused in the hallway before going into the living room, eavesdropping on the conversation between his wife and the babysitter.

It didn't take long for their private conversation to bring a sexy fantasy to mind, so he found a bottle of wine in the pantry and waited for the right moment to join them.

If his wife didn't take the bottle and asked him to serve her a glass, that would make him understand that she didn't want to; but... if she drank straight from the bottle, it meant that she was also into it.

Laura leaned closer to Katy, looked at the babysitter with genuine affection as she combed the girl's bangs with her fingers.

"Have you ever had an orgasm so intense it makes you shake from the tips of your toes to the tips of your hair?"

Katy took another sip from the bottle, the wine warming her body and relaxing her. The babysitter thought for a moment and then pressed her lips together shaking her head.

"I've have good orgasms, but I don't know if I would describe them that way."

"If you can't describe them like that, it's because you haven't had one like that." Laura leaned back, leaning her back on the armrest of the couch. "Chris gives the best orgasms I've ever had in my life," she said mischievously.

Katy was speechless, unsure of what to say now that he was with them in the living room.

Chris simply smirked. "Thanks, babe. You too." He winked at Katy before reaching out for her to pass the wine bottle.

Laura then asked her babysitter, "Have you ever had a threesome?"

Katy opened her eyes wide as saucers as she felt her insides melt. Had she heard correctly?

"No," she answered in a small voice, feeling the blush of embarrassment and excitement creep up her cheeks.

Laura looked at her husband with complicity and returned her gaze to the babysitter, her face wore a sensual expression, like a feline about to capture her prey.

"Would you like to have a threesome with us?"

Katy watched her and nodded shyly.

Laura slowly approached the beautiful young woman on her hands and knees. Katy watched as the attractive and experienced woman approached her, her breasts hanging like provocative fruit from her torso, revealing the weight of her breasts and her deep cleavage. She felt her breath on her lips before closing her eyes, her heart pounding in her chest and an explosion of sensation assailing her when those soft lips touched hers, kissing her like no one ever had before.

Chris watched excitedly as his wife seduced the babysitter. The figures of both women contrasting, his wife and her voluptuous curves that never stopped driving him crazy, and the babysitter with her nubile figure, hungry to know and discover what her body was capable of, seducing the couple with her smooth skin, perky tits and tight little ass.

Katy moaned against Laura's lips, her hands tangled in her long hair while the older woman touched the babysitter's tits over her shirt. Between kisses and intertwined tongues they undressed each other, remaining only in their underwear, while Chris had already stripped down to his boxers, he gripped his hard cock, stroking himself as he watched his wife and babysitter make out and touch each other, exploring their bodies with curious hands and mouths.

The red lace underwear contrasted against her skin, hugging her curves; Katy couldn't deny the desire she felt to tug at the cups that held her big, round tits. When her fingers rolled the thin fabric down, she gazed at her erect nipples.

She ran her tongue around the curve of one breast, reaching her peak, wrapping it between her lips and sucking on it. She moaned when she felt a thin spray of sweet liquid land on her tongue. Of course! Laura still breastfed her youngest, and her breasts were deliciously full of milk.

Her other nipple started dripping when Katy had triggered her let-down reflex by sucking on her breast.

"It tastes so good!" the babysitter said licking her lips and latching on the the other breast that was overflowing. "It's so sweet!" she said after gulping down another mouthful of creamy milk.

Laura moaned and pressed the babysitter's face against her chest, the young girl had her dripping wet all around, she could feel the slickness of her arousal flooding her panties.

Katy squeezed her soft flesh, making her tips overflow with cream. Fine jets of milk sprayed from her nipples, leaving a trail of white pearl like drops across the babysitter's face.

Then Laura looked at her husband, her eyes twinkling with lust. She reached out her arm for him to come closer. Chris walked around the couch and brought his stiff member to the face of his wife, who immediately received him by opening her mouth and sucking his thick cock.

Laura moved her head back and forth, hungrily sucking on her husband's cock. Katy felt excited upon seeing that he approached them to participate in the threesome.

"Why don't you come and suck his cock while I

lick his balls, hun." Laura had released his length and the babysitter stopped nursing from her milk filled tits to now put another woman's husband's cock in her mouth.

Chris gasped with pleasure, his sex throbbing as two soft mouths and tongues indulged in licking, and sucking the most sensitive parts of him.

It was a delicious and naughty fantasy come true, watching and feeling his wife and the babysitter take turns sharing his cock between their mouths.

"Who wants me to fuck her?" asked Chris, looking at both women.

"I want to watch you fuck Katy. I want to see how you bury your cock inside her tight little pussy and make her writhe in pleasure! Show her what a real man feels like in her pussy and then show her how good it feels when you fuck her ass."

The babysitter ended up on her back on the couch, Laura's tits hanging over her, small drops of her sweet milk dripping in her mouth and on her face while her husband slid her white panties down her thighs. Her shaved pussy was pink and juicy. He grabbed her by her hips and positioned himself between her legs, his bulbous head pressing against her folds. They both held their breath when he barely pushed the tip of his cock into her. The tight embrace of her sex engulfed him inch by inch, until his hard cock was buried to the hilt, deep into her nubile channel.

As he pulled out his length, his cock glistened with her juices, the babysitter was soaking wet while he and his wife continued to show her how good she could feel between the two of them.

With each thrust, Katy sucked on Laura's tits harder, she couldn't believe how turned on she was by sucking her milk filled tits.

"Oh baby girl, that feels so good!" Laura crooned, feeling her clit throb each time the babysitter sucked the milk from her nipples. "Now I'm going to sit on your face while my husband fucks you, I want you to make me cum with that naughty mouth!"

Katy moaned, desperate to consume and be consumed by this sensually perverse couple.

Laura straddled her face and lowered her wet slit to the babysitter's mouth. Katy breathed in her aroused feminine fragrance; it was the first time that she had been intimate with a woman, and everything they had done so far just made her wanton for more. She kissed her folds before tracing her tongue between them; she lapped at the older woman's pussy, licking and drinking her juices with an obscene appetite.

The babysitter tongued her clit while her husband thrust his cock it in and out of the young woman with a relentless rhythm that brought her ever closer to the brink of ecstasy.

Laura rode her face, rubbing her sex over her mouth. Chris delighted in groping his wife's large tits, which swayed in time with the movements of her body. He massaged her breasts with both hands and then pinched around her nipples, making them spray fine jets of milk that landed on his toned chest and the babysitter's perky breasts and flat belly. He thrust deeply into the Katy's pussy and leaned over to kiss his wife fully on the lips, enjoying the feel of having the nubile babysitter caught between them.

His hands were wet with her warm milk. Chris then groped the babysitters' smaller breasts, rubbing his wife's breast milk onto her skin and pinching her smaller nipples. Katy moaned against Laura's pussy, but when Chris started rubbing her clit, her moans grew more desperate and her licking became frenzied.

"Oh yeah! Keep eating my pussy just like that, baby girl!" Laura moaned while rubbing herself harder, riding and fucking the babysitter's face. "You're going to make me cum!"

She felt the vibrations of Katy moaning loudly against her pussy, the babysitter's body trembling, seized by an intense orgasm that triggered her own climax. Chris required all of his self-control so as not to empty himself into the babysitter, since the vision of the two women cumming had his balls tightly clenched and ready to shoot his load.

Chris was still harder than a rock when Laura lay down next to Katy, still impaled by her husband, and kissed her lips, the girls mouth and chin smeared with her juices while she caressed the young woman's breasts. When Katy caught her breath she only said, "God! That was the most intense orgasm of my life!"

"Yet..." Chris added with a mischievous tone and flexed his member inside her, causing another spasm of pleasure.

"Come and lie down, Chris. For her first time from behind she will feel better if she rides you."

Chris pulled out his cock, which was streaked white with her cum and lay down where moments ago Katy had lain. His fat cock surged between his legs, while he waited for her virginal ass to impale herself on his member.

Laura was gone for a moment and returned with a lubricant that she spread generously over her husband's length and then rubbed the viscous liquid between the babysitter's ass cheeks, but not before penetrating her slit with a lubricated finger and rubbing her clit, making the young woman gasp.

The babysitter was crouched over her husband, with her back to his face as Laura had indicated.

"Spread your ass cheeks, baby girl. And start going down, I'll help guide you."

Katy nodded, eager to feel more of everything she was experiencing with the two of them.

Her slender body kneeled on top of Chris, her

small hands parted her round ass cheeks, and there between her buttocks was the dark circle of her anus.

Chris held his sex like a dagger, firm and positioned to penetrate her virginal asshole.

Laura gently guided her hips, helping her get right on target. As soon as the pink head of his cock touched her anus, she lowered herself little by little, pressing her lips together when his cockhead stretched out the tight skin of her sphincter.

It was a sensation like no other, her delicate skin burning with every inch that pushed into her, but despite that, she kept pushing down, impaling her ass on his thick cock.

Laura whispered words of comfort, encouraging her not to stop; she would soon feel better than she had ever imagined.

When his bulbous glans pierced through her ass, taking in his shaft was easier. She slowly managed to impale herself completely on Chris's sex, his hard cock buried deep in her rectum.

The fullness she felt from having her ass filled with his cock was overwhelming, she didn't know how they expected her to move with her ass so full.

"Just sit there, get used to the feeling," Laura whispered against her mouth before kissing her.

Laura's lips moved down her neck, reaching her small, perky breasts. She groped her tits, pinched her nipples, licking and sucking harder and harder until she heard the girl moan.

A hand slid down her belly until it reached the triangle of her sex, where she didn't hesitate to rub her hard little clit.

Laura sucked her tits and masturbated the babysitter while she sat on her husband, a whirlwind of pleasure made her forget the pain of feeling a hard cock stuffed in her ass, and where before she was not sure if she liked it, now she yearned for every inch buried in her tunnel.

Laura's caresses provoked a reaction in her body, she was consumed with desire, maddened by lust, and she was moving up and down on Chris's lap.

The more Laura rubbed her clit, the hornier she felt. Soon her ass cheeks were slapping against Chris, her tight little ass riding his length.

"I think Katy likes my cock in her ass, babe," Chris said, enjoying the young woman's excited rhythm.

"And you? Do you like to fuck our babysitter in the ass?"

"I love it!" he answered and gave her a loud spank.

"Do you like it, Katy? Do you like to feel my husband's hard cock buried in your ass?"

"Oh yes!" she moaned ecstatically while she bounced up and down, his fat cock stretching and filling her tight little anus. "Everything you've done to me feels so good!!"

"What if I suck her pussy while you fuck her in the ass?"

"If you keep talking like that, I won't be able to hold out much longer, babe. My balls are going to explode!"

His adored and nasty wife knelt on the floor, at the precise height where the babysitter and Chris's body were joined together.

"Do you want me to eat your pussy, baby girl?"

"Yes! Please! Please lick my pussy while your husband fucks my ass!!" She begged wantonly.

Laura licked between the babysitter's folds, connecting with her clit each time her ass slid down his cock.

Katy's moans became more desperate; she couldn't take so much pleasure. Laura tasted her juices, her tongue moving up and down her slit until she brought her hand up, and without warning, buried two fingers deep into her pussy, all the while wrapping her lips around her pulsing little clit and sucked softly on her sensitive nub.

"Oh my God! Oh my God! I'm cumming!!"

The babysitter's body jerked as if she were on a runaway steed, when in reality it was the involuntary sway of her own body consumed by her climax.

Her juices gushed from her pussy with the contractions of her body, dripping down Laura's hand; the provocative wife then focused on her husband's tight sack, she lowered her mouth to his balls. When she sucked on her husband's heavy balls, his muscles clenched and he shot his load deep into the babysitter's ass, filling her with his hot, sticky cum.

When the overwhelming pleasure of their orgasms stopped, the babysitter got off Chris's lap, both exhausted and satisfied. They then contemplated Laura, who was still kneeling on the floor.

"I think were not done with you yet, babe" Chris said looking at his wife.

"Always such a gentleman" Laura stood up and sat on the sofa with her legs spread. "I want you to suck me and finger me like you know how I like it while Katy sucks my tits."

The babysitter looked at her with a flirty smile and leaned towards Laura, squeezing her soft, round breasts and sucking on her nipples until she coaxed milk from them once again.

Her husband knelt on the floor between her legs and pushed his middle and index finger inside her slick pussy and his thumb pushed inside the tight ring of her anus. While he finger fucked his wife's ass and pussy, he leaned his face between her legs and licked her eager clit

Soon after, Laura was writhing on the couch,

pleasure climbing inside her as the babysitter sucked her hypersensitive tits, drinking the milk from her nipples while her husband went down on her, fingering her pussy and asshole. Her climax radiated from her core, consuming every cell in her body, reveling in the four hands and two mouths on her.

After their licentious encounter, the three of them drank some more wine before getting dressed. The couple said goodbye to their babysitter, each taking a turn to kiss her lips with intimate complicity, assuring her that they would soon see each other again.

THE END

Creamy 9
and Overflowing
Mami also
Wants Milk
Lesbian Lactation Erotica Short Story
Adriana Gala

Mami Also Wants Milk

Creamy and Overflowing 9

Sofia had moved with her family into the house next door two months ago, and in that short time we had become good friends. She was a first-time mother like me and our children were almost the same age. Her son Sergio is one year and nine months old, while my little Miguel is already one year and eight months old.

Today it was her turn to take the two boys to the nursery where they spent half a day playing with other babies and their teachers. Those hours were a needed break to be able to do things like grocery shopping, errands, housekeeping, and now, at Sofia's insistence, we also went to a gym a couple of times a week.

I walked to the door when the bell rang, Sofia had already returned from leaving the children and was dressed in black leggings with hot pink designs and a tight matching top, her long jet-black hair was fastened in a ponytail.

"Why are you still in your nightgown?" she asked.

The only thing I had done before getting Miguel ready that morning was brushing my teeth; I was so tired that I hadn't even breastfed him like I usually did. So it wasn't only that I was deeply disappointed about what happened last night with Antonio, my husband, but on top of that, my boobs felt like two concrete mountains on my chest.

"I really don't feel like going to the gym today, Sofi. I'd rather stay home if you don't mind."

"At least lets have a cup of coffee and tell me what's wrong," she said walking into the house and straight to the kitchen.

Sofia poured two cups, and passing me one she asked, "So, what happened that you have such a sad face?"

"It's nothing," I said with a wave of my hand. "I'm just overtired, that's all. I had a rough night."

My friend made a sympathetic gesture with her lips.

"Did Miguel not let you sleep last night?"

"No, he's actually sleeping really well to tell you the truth. It's just that…"

"What's wrong, Paola? You know you can tell me anything. *Vamos amiga*, let it out, that's what friends are for."

I didn't know how to say this out loud, let alone to another person…

"It's just that ever since I got pregnant and had Miguel, things with Antonio haven't been the same."

"You mean sex?"

I tightened my grip on the cup in my hands, feeling my cheeks turning warmer than the steaming coffee. I nodded apologetically.

"I'm very sorry, that must be a painful situation for you. Tell me what happened between you two; maybe I can give you some advice."

I raised my eyebrows in amazement. Here I was blushing like a schoolgirl talking about my sex life with my husband; and my new friend, who was a single mom living with her father, was handling the conversation with such confidence and tranquility as if we were swapping recipes.

"Well, the first thing I can tell you is," said Sofia, "put the shame aside. "What's more, send it off to another planet, because embarrassment in the bedroom brings more problems than fun."

"Easier said than done," I said. "How I wish I had your confidence."

"I'm not ashamed to feel pleasure, however naughty it may be. If we're consenting adults and we're not hurting anyone, we are entitled to freely enjoy ourselves and take pleasure from the most delicate and loving encounters to the wildest and most pornographic sex we are lucky enough to have."

A small smile crossed my face at Sofia's statement.

"I think you're right," I agreed. Right until she said it, I hadn't realized that the true anchor weighing our marriage down was the awkward embarrassment about how to approach each other now that my body had changed so drastically.

"But how do I get rid of the discomfort about how my body has changed? And how do I get Antonio to do the same?"

"First, you need to relax and stop thinking so much. The art of physical love is in feeling, not thinking."

"Okay, that makes sense," I said biting my lip.

"Come on, let's go to the living room. I'm going to teach you some breathing techniques so you can learn how to relax."

I smiled gratefully and we walked out of the kitchen.

Sofia told me to sit cross-legged on the carpet, she instructed me to keep my back straight but as relaxed as possible. She told me to close my eyes, to breathe in deeply and with each exhalation I should concentrate on relaxing my body, part-by-part, starting with my feet. While I was focusing on relaxing each part of my body, she had knelt behind me and started massaging my shoulders. I hadn't noticed the tension I had accumulated until I felt her small hands patiently loosening the knots in my muscles.

A few minutes later, there was a noticeable difference in my body and in my breathing when I realized that the fabric of my nightgown covering my chest felt cold and wet. My relaxation exercises plus the fact that I hadn't unloaded the milk in my breasts since the previous evening caused the excess fluid to leak from my nipples.

Sofia noticed the change in my breathing or something because she asked, "What happened, Paola? You were very calm and I can tell that something changed."

"I must've relaxed too much cause my breasts are leaking and my nightie is getting wet," I said opening my eyes.

"So? The same happens to me. See what I told you? You're overthinking everything. You need to let go and stop judging yourself. Doesn't it feel good for the milk to be spilling from your breasts? Don't you feel less pressure in your chest?"

"Yeah, you're right, it does feel good."

"From now on you are forbidden to think and question. You just have to feel."

"Okay," I said, closing my eyes again.

Sofia's delicate hands stopped massaging my shoulders to rub up and down my arms. The sensation was pleasant and I shivered at the touch of her hands caressing my skin. I was immersed in the delicious feeling when I noticed that her repetitive strokes had caused the straps from my nightie to slide down my shoulders and her hands wandered under the satiny cloth that covered my large, swollen breasts. My heart skipped a beat, only to speed up as her fingers caressed the curve of my breasts and then pressed from the back towards my taught nipples, drawing even more milk from my overloaded breasts.

"She's milking me," the thought flashed through my mind before I remembered that I had promised that I wouldn't overthink things and succumb to my feelings. So I concentrated on the feel of her fingers under the fabric, that direct contact with my skin that longed for those caresses.

The few times Antonio had dared touch my breasts I had felt a flash of erotic pleasure, but embarrassment and shame had clouded my ability to become aware that I liked it. So our encounters had been more mechanical and uncomfortable rather than passionate.

But at this moment, under Sofia's instruction, I was giving way to the sense of ecstasy that her delicate hands awakened by milking my swollen tits.

A soft moan escaped my lips as I pushed out my chest, inviting her to continue what she was doing. My tits had become huge with the pregnancy, so

Sofia's dainty hands barely cupped a third of my flesh. Nevertheless, the softness of her palms caressing me aroused a burning desire within me.

Her fingers cupped the lower curve of my breasts while her thumb traveled over the top; her destination was my nipple dripping my pearly white milk. The nightie was already soaked from the amount of milk she had pumped out, relieving me of the pressure, leaving them soft and malleable.

"It feels so good what you're doing to me, Sofi," I managed to whisper. I was submerged in an ocean of unexplored sensations, each wave taking me further away from the surface of reason, drawing me into the depths of decadence.

"If that feels good, this will feel even better," she said as I felt the absence of her hands milking my tits.

Moments later I felt her kneel between my legs.

My deep breathing had been replaced by panting; I was breathless, as if I were running a marathon even though I was still sitting on the floor of my living room. A surprised moan escaped my throat as I felt Sofia's tongue licking the tip of my nipple just before wrapping her lips around the stiffened peak.

I leaned back, bracing my weight with one hand while the other held my friend's head towards my bosom, pushing her face into the breast she was suckling.

My clit throbbed wantonly; my pussy was wet, leaving a sodden patch where I was sitting on my nightgown.

Sofia suckled my tit ravenously, greedily slurping milk that flowed from my body. Every time she sucked me, flashes of ecstasy tingled all over my skin. We both moaned, and as she pressed her face against my fleshy tit, my hips swayed, seeking contact with hers.

I opened my eyes; I was consumed with so much desire that I just wanted to feel more of her. She moved her head slightly from my breast and looked into my eyes. Her lust-filled stare revealed that she was just as turned on as I was.

"You're delicious, Paola," she said smiling before bringing her hungry lips down again and suckled my other breast with wanton hunger.

I tossed my head back while she drank my milk. My nightie had bunched up over my hips, leaving my sex uncovered and seeking to rub my naked pussy against her.

When her hand came between us I thought I would faint with pleasure. She slid her finger through my glistening lips, smearing her finger with my cream before penetrating my wet slit. She finger-fucked my pussy while never stopping from sucking on each of my tits, slurping so much milk from my nipples that it dripped down her chin.

I had enough self-control to beg her to stop, I was so close to coming that it was almost painful when she pulled her hand away from my hungry slit.

She looked at me uncertainly, but moments later I cast away her doubts by covering her lips with mine and kissing her deeply.

"I don't want to come yet," I whispered against her mouth. "And *Mami* also wants milk," I said before dipping my tongue into her mouth. I became drunk with the sweet taste that permeated her breath.

I made my way kissing down her neck until I reached her chest. I pulled her top off over her head together with her sports bra. My mouth watered when I looked upon her round mounds. I brought my face to her nipple, tentatively sticking my tongue out, tasting that tight bud, licking her softly. Sofia whimpered, but I just turned to her other breast and teased her nipple with little fluttering licks of my tongue.

"Please, Paola, please," she begged.

I opened my mouth and got as much of her generous flesh as I could and sucked hard. Another flash of ecstasy swept over me as I felt a stream of milk invade my mouth, flooding it with a deliciously sweet taste.

Now I was suckling her voraciously. I couldn't get enough of her sweet, creamy milk. I sucked and slurped her milky breasts with abandon. I only stopped for a minute to finish undressing. Now we were both completely naked. I opened my legs and straddled one of her thighs, both of us rubbing our sex against the other's leg while taking turns sucking on our full tits. When she suckled me, I held her head firmly against my chest and rocked my hips, rubbing my wet slit against her leg. Then I tilted my head to her beautiful tits loaded with the sweetest nectar I had ever tasted, sucking them hard, filling my mouth with her milk and seeking out hers to share her cream. We were covered and overflowing with our juices, the sweet liquid dripping from our breasts and the bitter nectar that oozed between our legs. Occasionally I would interrupt rubbing myself against her leg to push a finger inside myself, penetrating my wet slit, then bring that finger to our mouths, both tasting that sticky essence.

After drinking from her and filling my mouth to spill it over her naked body I said, "If I could eat your pussy and tits at the same time, I would. But now I want to drown myself with the cream of your slit."

We shifted our positions; our bare tits swaying with our movements until she was sitting on an armchair with her legs wide open, letting me gaze upon her wet pussy.

I buried my face between her legs, the bitter taste of her essence assaulting my palate with that pornographic flavor after having obscenely gorged myself with the sweet milk from her tits. I drew my tongue through her cleft, licking her from ass to clit, until I focused my swirling tongue straight onto that hard little pearl and started fucking her pussy with my finger as she had done with me.

My index finger was plunging in and out of her folds when she cried out, "More! Give me more!"

At her begging pleas I was now burying four fingers deep into her sex, fucking her pussy while I licked her pebbled clit. Her wetness dripped down my hand as she countered my movements with her hips.

"Eat my pussy, Paola! God! Yes! Suck my clit with your dirty mouth! I'm so close! I'm so close, *Mami*! I'm going to come!"

I fucked her pussy harder with my fingers while wrapping my lips around her pebbled clit and sucked.

I felt her slick channel clench around my hand as her hips convulsed with her climax. I moved my head to the rhythm of her spasms so as to not let go of her throbbing clit. She covered her mouth with her hand trying to drown out her ecstatic cries. Gradually, the rhythmic embrace of her sex slowed down, I released her clit when I felt her body jerking with aftershocks of pleasure.

She was panting, her bare breasts rising and falling with her breath. When she finally opened her eyes and looked at me she said, "Come here, *Mami*. Now I'm going to eat your pussy."

She got up from the chair and lay down on the carpet.

"Sit on my face, Paola."

I straddled her face, my dripping slit right above her lips. When I got close enough, a shiver ran through my body when her tongue tasted my pussy.

She clutched my ass with her hands, digging her fingers into the flesh of my hips that started moving of their own accord while I was riding her face. One of her hands slid down the crack of my ass until she reached my opening where she pushed three fingers at the same time into my pussy and fucked me again with her hand, all the while licking and sucking my clit.

The pleasure climbed and climbed its way to the peak. I couldn't stop moaning as I rubbed my pussy against her face and squeezed my tits, causing jets of milk to burst out of my nipples, soaking my hands, my chest and my abdomen with that white liquid.

I was riding her face wildly, completely overcome with what she was doing to me with her fingers and tongue until the orgasm slammed into my body with a fulminating force that made my legs buckle and had me brace myself with my hands on the floor so as not to fall over from the violent jolts of my climax. But even in this position, her relentless mouth didn't stop working my throbbing clit, ripping a keening wail from my throat.

Even though I had already reached the peak of my climax, my body wouldn't obey me. My hands and knees were on the floor on top of Sofia and my hips didn't stop rocking back and forth on her velvety tongue. She grabbed me hard by the ass with both hands and used the cadence of my hips to set the pace of her licking. Before I knew it, another violent orgasm shook my body, ripping ecstatic cries from my throat while stealing my breath away.

Sofia did this to me three more times, until I was begging her to stop. I couldn't take any more pleasure; only then did she let me lay down beside her. She hugged my body, her curves molding to mine. We lay naked on the floor of the living room, I was still catching my breath from the most intense sexual experience of my life when she traced her fingers up my belly to my chest; she squeezed one of my nipples, where immediately a drop of white milk formed. "You see why it's more important to feel than to think when you make love?" She said before covering my lips with a delicate kiss that was loaded with the promise that this was just our first time.

THE END

Short Stories Available on Kindle

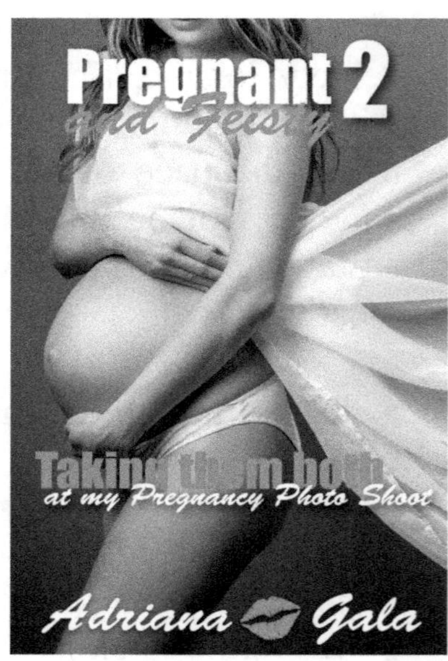